Zombie Diaries

Homecoming Junior Year

The Mavis Saga

By
R.W.K. Clark

Published in the United States by Clarkltd.
Po Box 45313 Rio Rancho, NM 87174
info@clarkltd.com

Edition 1

United States Copyright Office
#TX 8-393-550 April 2017
Library of Congress Control Number: 2017907165
International Standard Book Numbers
ISBN-10: 0997876778
ISBN-13: 978-0997876772
ASIN: B071DVTHKL

/200801

ZOMBIE DIARIES SERIES

Zombie Diaries - Homecoming Junior Year - ZD1
ISBN-10: 0997876778 ISBN-13: 978-0997876772

Zombie Diaries - Winter Formal Junior Year - ZD2
ISBN-10: 0997876786 ISBN-13: 978-0997876789

Zombie Diaries - Prom Junior Year - ZD3
ISBN-10: 0997876794 ISBN-13: 978-0997876796

Zombie Diaries - Summer Break Junior Year - ZD4
ISBN-10: 1948312034 ISBN-13: 978-1948312035

Zombie Diaries - Fall Semester Senior Year - ZD5
ISBN-10: 1948312042 ISBN-13: 978-1948312042

Zombie Diaries - Senior Graduation - ZD6
ISBN-10: 1948312050 ISBN-13: 978-1948312059

CONTENTS

ACKNOWLEDGMENTS

I dedicate this novel to my wonderful readers and for all the amazing people I've met and those I haven't. To my family and loved ones, all your support will not be forgotten.

This book was made possible by reviews from readers like you.

Thank you

R.W.K. Clark

CHAPTER 1

Mavis Harvey reclined lazily on the family sofa, one leg resting on the backrest, a shoe dangling from her toes. Both of her arms were thrown up over her head, and her other foot tapped to the poppy tune pumping out of the television speaker. She loved this show: *The Cravens.* It was about a family of nerds, with the exception of one daughter, who just happened to be the hippest, most popular girl at her high school. Mavis often daydreamed that her life would be more like that of Carrie Craven on the show.

As it was, Mavis was pretty much your average, everyday teenage high school girl. Almost seventeen, she liked boys, but as of yet, she had failed to gain the attention of the opposite sex at all. She was limited to her daydreams and hopes for the future. Hopes of changing from what she considered to be an ugly duckling into a beautiful swan, and gaining the attention of boys.

It didn't help that she was pretty down-to-Earth. She wasn't a 'Barbie girl,' as she called them. Her hair wasn't perfect, and she didn't pile on the makeup. Mavis Harvey was about as real as one could get. With Mavis,

there were no false pretenses or masks. She was just...
Mavis.

Her best friend was Kim Coleman. Kim was a pretty girl who carried just a bit too much weight. She was funny and smart, but she did depend on makeup and hair to balance the scales of her love for all things food. Mavis didn't care how Kim looked. She believed that someday, they both would blossom and surprise every last idiot at Westside High, especially every girl who had pointed and snickered at them when they'd walked by.

Mavis lived in Greenville, a small suburb of Toledo. She had lived there her entire life; in fact, her mother and father had bought their home when Mavis had been only eighteen months old. She was a very content, happy, and well-adjusted teenager, with goals, ambitions, and dreams.

A commercial came on, and Mavis put both of her feet on the floor. She was hungry. It was two o'clock on Saturday afternoon, and they wouldn't eat until six. Jumping up, she raced to the kitchen and, in a hurry to get back to *The Cravens*, blindly grabbed a fresh bag of chips and jogged back to the sofa just as the commercial ended.

Carrie Craven was bringing a boy home for the first time ever, but he wasn't just any boy; no, this one was the captain of the football team. Carrie was embarrassed by her family's nerdiness, so before he came, she was trying to make them all cool. This Carrie character was one of the 'Barbie girls' that were so unlike Mavis and Kim. In this episode, her entire family was running around the house like chickens with their heads cut off, trying to do and be what their daughter wanted them to do and be for this guy she was dating, and Mavis thought it was hilarious. She laughed loudly as she opened her chips automatically grabbing one and popping it into her mouth.

Suddenly, her eyes went wide; the chips were burning hot, seasoned with some kind of pepper. Jumping up, Mavis ran for the kitchen and grabbed the first glass she saw out of the dish drainer. With a quick turn of the knob, she filled the glass with water and proceeded to gulp it down. After a moment, she knew it wouldn't be enough.

Mavis held the glass out to refill it but immediately stopped. The water coming from the tap was now brown, and a bit snotty-looking. The water in her glass had been clear, and a smack of her lips told her it tasted normal, overall. Maybe a slight dirt taste, but nothing she would have ever noticed if she hadn't seen the sludge oozing from the tap. She stared into the depths of the glass, but the few drops of water inside appeared to be clear.

"Mom! Dad!" Mavis left the water running and yelled around the corner and down the hallway. "Something is wrong with this water! It's all gross and stuff!" Her father's head popped out of their bedroom door. "What? What do you mean, gross?"

Mavis shrugged and rolled her eyes. "I don't know, Dad. It's all brown and stuff. Like, dirty, you know?"

Todd Harvey stepped out of the doorway and

started up the hall, his wife Jane right on his heels. He was dressed for the day in blue jeans and a polo shirt; his wife was clutching a robe around her body, and a towel was wrapped like a turban on her head.

"I just got out of the shower ten minutes ago, Mavis and the water was fine," she scolded.

Ten seconds later the three of them stood before the double-panned kitchen sink, staring at the muck which was shooting out of the tap. It was thicker now, and still brown, but there were tinges of green here and there as well.

"See?" Mavis muttered. "I told you so. Gross."

Todd took a coffee cup from the drainer and caught some of the muddy mess in it. He held it up to his nose, took a brief whiff, and jerked his head back, a sour, disgusted look on his face. Mavis could almost see the wheels turning in his head as he tried to figure out what the heck was going on.

"Well, Todd?" Jane asked. "What is it?"

He shrugged and set the cup aside, then turned off the tap and plucked his cell phone out of his pocket. I have no idea, but nobody drink this water until I get the plumber over here, got it?" He turned to Mavis. "You didn't drink this, did you?"

She gave him a surprised look. "Dad! That's disgusting! Actually, I filled a glass, and the water was fine. I drank it and went to fill it again, and the water was like this; it happened just like that."

Todd looked her over, contemplating. "Did it taste bad?"

"No."

"Okay," he continued. "Well, no more. I'm calling Ralph to come to take a look at it. Back to your business, everyone."

Mavis and her mother exchanged a brief glance before leaving the kitchen and going their separate ways, Mavis back to the television, and Jane to her room to finish dressing. As soon as she plopped down on the couch, however, Mavis realized she had completely missed the rest of *The Cravens*; she groaned and flopped back in annoyance before grabbing the remote and beginning the search for new entertainment.

After a moment, she found some reruns of *Rock and Roll High School*, another popular program for teens her age. She put the remote on the coffee table and settled in, her father's voice echoing slightly from the kitchen as he spoke to Ralph, the plumber. Mavis barely let it register, though. She was feeling a bit as though a nap might be a good idea. What a lazy Saturday.

"Mavis, wake up."

Her eyes fluttered open to see her mother bending over the back of the sofa, leaning toward her daughter. "What? What do you want? I was sleeping."

Jane put her palm flat on her daughter's forehead. "You're covered in sweat! Are you feeling okay?"

Suddenly, Mavis was very aware of the sweat; she was covered in it, her shirt even soaked clear through. She struggled to sit up. "Yeah, I am all sweaty," she muttered as she plucked the material of her top away from her skin. "Must be super-hot in here, Mom. Turn the heat down."

Jane turned to the thermostat on the wall. "The heat isn't on, Mavis. You need to go take some medicine and put yourself to bed."

Suddenly, the girl was wide awake. "Bed? I thought we were going to eat out. Prime rib? I know what's going on." She reached up and poked her mother playfully. "You want my share. I see how it is."

Taking her daughter by the arm to help her up, Jane shook her head. "Stop being silly." Jane felt her head and knit her brow. "You don't seem to have a fever. You're sure you're feeling all right? I sure hope that water didn't throw your system off somehow."

She began to steer the girl down the hall to her room, and even though Mavis felt fine, she didn't fight it. If she was honest, she did feel a little bit woozy, even though her appetite was in full raging force.

"No, we aren't going for prime rib," Jane replied, opening Mavis' bedroom door and pulling back her blankets. She put her daughter in the bed and pulled the blankets up under her chin, then flipped on the small flat-screen hanging on Mavis' wall. "We have to wait for Ralph to come about the water. We'll eat here. Are you really hungry? Because, to be honest, you look like death warmed over."

Mavis let her mother tuck her in. "I'm starving! Promise to wake me up when it's time to eat, please Mom?"

Jane gave her daughter a kiss on the forehead and smoothed her hair back. "You don't seem to have a fever. Just rest up, and as soon as it's time for supper I'll come get you, okay?"

With a loving look, Mavis smiled and closed her eyes. Her mother was right, perhaps; she did feel tired, and even a bit dizzy. It was much cooler in her room, even with the blankets on, which made it easy to get comfortable, and before long she was snoring lightly and beginning a new dream.

She dreamed about being the most popular girl in school, like Carrie Craven on TV. She was going to bring home a boy, and she didn't want her dork family to embarrass her. While the story played out behind her closed eyes, Mavis smiled.

R.W.K. Clark

CHAPTER 2

"Anyway, it was super-gross, like runny brown poop coming out of the faucet. I think it upset my stomach or something because I felt like crap for a little bit, I feel much better now. The plumber said it looks like a rat made it into the pump."

"Disgusting," Kim spat.

Mavis was reclining on her bed, the cordless house phone to her ear and both of her feet on the posts of her bed at the foot. She had a canopy bed that her grandmother had given her the year before; it was an antique and made her feel like a princess. She loved it.

"I'm grossed out," her best friend, Kim said. "Then you'll be in school Monday right? Have you thought about the dance?" The homecoming game and dance were quickly approaching, and it was the highlight of the first quarter at school for everyone.

Mavis groaned internally. Had she thought about the dance? That was all she ever thought about! She daydreamed endlessly that someone from school, maybe the ultra-hot Jeff Deason, would ask her at the last minute to go. But Mavis knew she wasn't popular with the boys at all. As a matter of fact, she was pretty sure that not a single boy at Westside High even knew she existed.

"Yeah, yeah. I've thought about it." She rolled over onto her stomach and began to pick lint off one of her teddy bears. "I just don't know if I can handle the embarrassment of going stag two years in a row, Kim."

Her friend grunted. "Well, if I'm with you, and we're both going alone, then we're not really going alone, are we?"

Kim and Mavis had attended each and every dance together, without dates, since they began their school careers. That included the Sadie Hawkins dance in eighth grade, a dance which focused on the girls asking the boys. That year, they had each asked a boy, and they had each been shot down in flames. Neither of them was willing to take a hit a second time, and they simply went together dancing eating brownies and drinking punch.

Mavis shook her head at Kim's reasoning. "Fine, we'll go with the usual plan. Look, I'm starving. I'm going to get something to eat and watch some TV before bed. Call me tomorrow, okay?"

The girls hung up, and Mavis glanced at her bedside clock: ten-thirty. Her parents would be in their room watching the late show so she would have the big television in the living room to herself. She rose and made her way to her parents' room, where she rapped lightly on the door.

"Yes?"

Mavis opened the door a crack and popped her head

in. "I think I got too much rest today," she told them with a smile. "I'm going to go watch TV and have a snack if that's okay."

Her mother's brow creased. "You ate like a horse at supper. You're hungry again?"

"Just a little," Mavis said with a shrug. "I feel fine. Just can't sleep."

Now Todd gave her a grunt. "Don't go out, and don't unlock any of the doors for any reason. Oh, and don't let me find you sleeping on that couch, Mavis. It's bad for your back. It will give you scoliosis and cause you to have chronic headaches. Do you know the price of a back brace, or even migraine medicines, nowadays?"

Mavis rolled her eyes but agreed. "Sure thing, Dad."

She made a peanut butter and jelly, gave the faucet a glance, shook her head, and poured a glass of milk. Ralph had come over and taken care of the problem. The water was running clean, but she didn't want to take a risk. It made her feel a bit funny the first time, and she wasn't willing to go through that again quite so soon.

Mavis settled on watching an 'adult' cartoon while she ate. She lay back and got comfortable, but she didn't focus on the show. She wound up daydreaming about Jeff Deason once again, the most popular and good-looking boy in school. What would it be like to get asked to the dance by him? Just the thought gave her goosebumps. But she knew that before a boy asked a girl, he should probably know her name, and Mavis was willing to bet money that he didn't. Oh, well, it wouldn't be the first homecoming dance she went to with Kim.

Maybe, for once in her life, she should take a risk and ask him. Sure, it wasn't the traditional thing to do when it came to homecoming, but she had never seen him with a girl, and he didn't really seem to chase anyone around. As a matter of fact, he was always with his friends, with girls throwing themselves at him and embarrassing themselves. Maybe she should step out of her comfort zone. While the idea was entertaining, and even seemed feasible from the comfort of her living room, Mavis knew that it was nothing more than a pipe dream. By the time she woke up in the morning the light bulb over her head wouldn't have just burned out, it would be cracked and broken.

It wasn't long before she began to doze off, and it took a lot of effort for her to shut off the TV and get to her room so she wouldn't get scolded for sleeping on the couch in the morning. Tomorrow she would call Kim, and they would decide what they should wear to the stupid homecoming dance. They should at least match.

So, for the second time that day, Mavis fell into a deep, comfortable sleep.

∞

"Mom, after breakfast I'm going to Kim's house to go online and get some ideas for homecoming dresses."

Mavis was shoveling her food into her mouth at breakneck speed. Both Todd and Jane watched her, their mouths open and their eyes wide. Neither of them had ever seen their daughter put away so much at once; she was a mere wisp of a girl. But for breakfast, she had taken three fried eggs, four strips of bacon, a pile of hash browns covered with cheese, and four slices of French toast. As they watched she ate the last bite and began to scrape up the syrup and yolk with the edge of her fork.

"Are you still hungry, Mavis?" her mother asked in a low voice.

Mavis looked at her as if she had grown a second head. "No," she replied, finally setting her fork down. "So, did you hear me? About the dress?"

Jane nodded. "Are you going to be going with a date this year, dear?"

"As of this moment, the answer is yes: Kim." Mavis stood and rinsed off her plate, then placed it in the dishwasher. "We want to match, like usual. What time will lunch be?"

Jane and Todd exchanged bewildered looks. Lunch? The girl had just almost cleaned the place out of breakfast food not three minutes ago! Usually, it was like pulling teeth to get her to clean her plate, and now she had just polished off enough food for a high school linebacker!

"Well," Jane finally replied, pulling herself together, "let us know if some lucky boy approaches you. It will happen any day now, you know."

An eye roll, hidden from their sight, was all she had to offer them. "Yeah. I know. Gotta go, see you soon."

R.W.K. Clark

CHAPTER 3

Mavis had been friends with Kim nearly her entire life. They met in kindergarten, and as it turned out, Kim, her mom, dad, and older brother Kenny lived only a block and a half away from Mavis. The two hit it off right away, and to her, Kim was like the sister Mavis never had.

It was a beautiful day; warm, but not too hot, and a nice breeze was blowing. Mavis had grabbed her jacket when she left the house, but now she held the nylon windbreaker in hand, thrown over her shoulder. As she neared the first corner, she saw that a group of boys were hanging out at a picnic bench in the park, located kitty-corner from where she was standing.

"Oh, my," Mavis muttered to herself. "Jeff Deason's over there!"

Her knees got all rubbery, and her hands started to shake. Were they walking in her direction? Oh, they were! Mavis began to glance around wildly and finally decided to pretend she didn't see them. They began to cross the street toward the same corner she had been aiming for. When she suddenly turned left and walked in the opposite direction from Kim's house.

"Are they laughing at me?" Now she spoke in a low voice, somewhat confident that she was out of earshot. "Wow! I think they are laughing at me!" She wanted to die. Why did she have to be so awkward and goofy?

Mavis crossed the street, glancing back at the boys as she did. They were a full block away now, and she was forgotten, if they had even noticed her, to begin with. But she was sure they had, and she felt like a moron for dodging them right in front of their faces.

Doubling back, she finally got to her friend's just five minutes later. They got comfortable in the girl's room, cross-legged on the floor, with a laptop open before them. Kim was pulling up the internet to look at dresses.

"They probably didn't even notice," the girl was saying as she typed. "So, you took an abrupt left in the middle of the block in front of the single most gorgeous boy in school. I think it's typical; he probably thought you just needed to turn left."

Mavis smirked at her friend. "Ha, ha. I'm pretty sure they were laughing at me, Kim. I could hear them."

Kim crinkled up her nose; she had a cute, round face, which fit her short, round body. She was adorable, and she was a good friend to Mavis. Unfortunately, her love for all things sugar seemed to affect the way boys looked at her.

"If they were laughing at you, at least they noticed you," she continued. "If they did, then Jeff did!"

"Do you think?" Mavis sat forward with excitement. This was true! If his friends noticed, he noticed, even if it was for a laugh.

Kim shrugged.

Mavis sat back against the bed, a starry look in her eyes. Then, a split-second later, she seemed to snap out of it. "Do you have anything to eat?"

Kim stopped scrolling and gave her friend a weird look. "Didn't you say you were going to finish eating and come right over when I talked to you on the phone earlier?" She paused.

Mavis nodded and cringed. "I did. But I feel like I haven't had a bite in days. Come on, let's go grab the cookies or something."

Kim stood up. "I guess you can afford it; what do you weigh, fifty pounds and all?"

"Funny."

Once Kim returned with some cookies, and a glass of milk to boot, they sat down and got to business with their dress shopping. Mavis gave Kim a look when she wouldn't take a cookie, but the girl simply smirked and patted her belly: dieting again.

Surprisingly they found what they wanted, and at a great price, too. Matching knee-length baby doll dresses in a fitted bodice, adorable in silver and black, with spaghetti straps. They both had a pair of black heels to match already, but by the time the dance rolled around they were sure to have a new pair each.

When they were finished, Mavis burped into her hand and groaned. "I suppose I should be getting home for lunch."

"You just ate a package of cookies." Kim handed

her a piece of paper with the dress information on it. "Make sure your mom gets on this, Mav. At the rate, you're eating you might wanna think about getting a bigger size."

Mavis stood and picked up the empty package, tossing it in the wastebasket. With the folded paper Kim gave her tucked firmly in her pocket, she grabbed her milk glass and headed for the door. Kim watched her, smiling.

"I'll rinse this out," Mavis said. "I'll have Mom get the dress right away. Don't go shoe shopping without me, because I know you're gonna."

"I won't. Call me later."

Mavis pretty much raced home for lunch, this time taking no notice of anything or anyone around her. She was going to be mellow for the rest of the day; back to school tomorrow, after all. For a second she thought about seeing Jeff and acting a fool, but she realized that she didn't care. As a matter of fact, she wanted to laugh about it. But that wasn't important right now, she just didn't want to miss lunch.

∞

Sunday afternoons and evenings were spent with Grandma Cabot. Every week, Mavis and her parents would head over there, help her crazy grandma around the house, and get treated to a wonderful meal. This Sunday was no exception.

They ended up helping her clean out the attic. It was a dirty, dusty job, but Grandma Cabot made it worthwhile with her crazy jokes. After about two hours, the four of them had the place looking as tip-top as an attic could look, and her grandmother was thankful.

"Tonight, we're having lamb chops, mashed potatoes and gravy, and mixed vegetables," she told them. She had been running up and down from the attic to the kitchen and back to get the meal ready while they cleaned. "And for dessert, warm peach cobbler and ice cream."

Mavis was starving, or at least she felt that way. Her stomach growled so loudly that both of her parents had been making fun of her while they worked. But now, it was doing more than growling, it was screaming for dear life. She practically ran to get to the kitchen, leaving her parents behind with curious looks on their faces and thoughts in their heads.

It was during dinner that Mavis' appetite grabbed her grandmother's attention and took it for a ride.

"May I have some more?" she asked after cleaning her plate for the second time.

The adults all looked at each other. Grandma Cabot was the one who spoke up. "Mavis, that will be your third complete helping. I hope you are watching your weight, girly."

"Mom," Jane said, "Mavis has always been thin, and we all know she had never eaten like this in her life. She must be needing the food." She turned to her daughter. "What's going on? Are you sure you want another plate?"

Mavis nodded.

"Well," her grandma sighed, "This is the last chop.

There are plenty more potatoes, and the veggies are gone. You had better save room for dessert."

Mavis put the last of the food on her plate and dug in. It was so delicious; it seemed as though she could taste flavors so keenly, better than ever before, and she just couldn't get enough. As for dessert, little did they know that if they weren't careful, she'd polish that all off, too.

The three adults watched as Mavis cleaned up every last bit of supper from the table, their mouths open and their eyes wide. When she was finished, Grandma Cabot simply gave a shrug and piled cobbler on her plate, along with a big scoop of vanilla ice cream. Mavis barely looked up long enough to thank her. She took the spoon her grandmother offered her and tore into the sweet treat.

Jane stared at her daughter, amused, then looked at the other two and shrugged.

"Teenagers," she said. "Who can figure them out?"

CHAPTER 4

"So, did you finish that report on photosynthesis?"

Mavis and Kim maneuvered their way through the crowded, noisy first-floor hallway of Westside High School. Kim had to yell to ask the question, and because of the pre-class chaos going on around them, Mavis had to wait to answer until they got to her locker. Kim's was on the second floor, so they always went to Mavis' first.

While entering her combination, Mavis replied, "Yeah, and it really turned me green!"

The two girls burst out in laughter, Mavis swinging her locker door open and stuffing her purse and books inside. Her first class was Literature, and she was fishing for her copy of *Passage of Time*. She had finished it a week ago, but Mrs. Lars always made the class read the assigned book until the due date that she had set, in this case, a week from today. So, Mavis had obliged by simply starting the book over again. She didn't mind at all; it was an awesome book, and it had really touched her heart. Besides, who knew what she would discover she missed the first time around?

"Well," Kim continued, "I guess I'll see you in science then. Are you going to walk me to my…?"

When her voice faltered, Mavis gave her a look. Kim was looking at something behind Mavis, and her mouth was open slightly. After a moment, the girl pulled herself out of her daze and nodded slightly.

"Never mind," she suddenly said with a slight smile. She turned to walk away, saying, "I can walk myself. See you in science, Mav."

She watched, confused, as Kim walked away, stunned at the girl's sudden change of attitude. What the heck had that been about? Shaking her head, Mavis grabbed *Passage of Time*, her binder, and her science book, then slammed her locker shut.

She quickly turned to head to the stairs for the second floor and Literature. She was so distracted that she nearly ran headlong into Jeff. He had been standing there, watching her all along, and Mavis quickly deduced that he had been the one who put Kim in such an odd state.

As soon as she saw him, Mavis dropped her books on the floor with such a loud bang that half the kids milling around her went silent and looked in her direction. She felt herself turning red; yep, no wonder Kim had skedaddled the way she had! Mavis made a mental note to kill her best friend right away upon leaving the school that afternoon. She would put her in a headlock and make her beg for mercy, then she would drag the girl to her house and make her give up every last cookie in the place.

She started to bend down for her books, but Jeff beat her to it, and the pair knocked heads fairly hard on the way down.

"Ow!" they exclaimed in unison, standing up and holding their respective sore spots. Jeff laughed, and when he was sure she wasn't going to try again, he stooped and fetched her books for her.

"Thank you," she muttered shyly. "Sorry about your head."

Mavis looked at the young man and almost immediately turned to jelly. His longish blond hair hung shaggily across his forehead in the latest style. His blue eyes were smiling. She realized, almost right away, that she didn't seem to be falling apart in front of him like most girls did. She always thought she would if she ever got face to face with him, or if they spoke. In her mind, if this day ever came, she would fall apart into a million pieces and wind up a blubbering pile of body parts on the floor.

"I saw you walking yesterday," he said lightly as she took her books from him. "Um, I hope you weren't embarrassed to walk by the guys and me. I mean, it kind of looked like you were avoiding us. I wouldn't have razzed you or anything, and I wouldn't have let any of those boneheads razz you either, you know."

Mavis began to shake her head. "No, no. I was just in a hurry to get to my friend's house, that's all. We had a busy morning planned. She didn't want me to be late."

"You mean Kim Coleman?" he asked. "I thought she lived in the opposite direction from the way you turned."

Mavis blushed because he had caught her lie. Could

she be any more of a moron? All she could think of to do was shrug and smile.

She began to slowly inch away from him and walk away, stumped as to what to offer to the light conversation. Jeff followed her though, and it made her so tense she thought she might snap in two. What was he doing, anyway? Mavis noticed that all kinds of kids were watching them, girls and boys, alike. Girls were pointing, some giggling and some sneering. Many had tried to conquer Mount Jeff, and here she was, a good ten feet up from the foot of it. She decided the best course of action was to ignore them, or their behavior would cause her to run and hide.

"What's your first class?" he asked as they walked.

"Literature," she replied.

The halls were quieting quickly now. "Oooh. Literature for homeroom… ugh, I have Social Studies, which, in its own way, is a hundred times worse. I'll walk you. Do you mind?"

Mavis glanced up at the perfect-looking young man and saw that he was smiling down at her. She smiled back, but even to her, it felt awkward and goofy. What the heck was going on? Had the Earth lined up with Jupiter or something?

"Um, sure. I guess." She shifted her books in her arms as they headed up the stairs.

"I can carry those for you, if you'd like," Jeff suggested.

She stopped, surprised, then timidly handed over the books. "Thanks."

"No problem," he replied, and the two began walking again.

Jeff cleared his throat, and for a fraction of a second Mavis wondered if he was as nervous as she was. The sound of clearing his throat made her think so, and she found herself relaxing a little. If he was nervous, even a little, she didn't feel so alone in her emotions. After all, he might be the best-looking, most popular boy in school, but he was human, too.

When they got to her class, Jeff stopped, "Look, do you want to hang out sometime? If you're not busy... or don't have a boyfriend."

Right away she took notice of the drop in the tone of his voice. Was he figuring her situation out? If he was, she could hardly believe it. Maybe it was some kind of joke, a prank his buddies had put him up to. Could Jeff Deason, her crush of Westside High, really be trying to find out if Mavis has a boyfriend? She could hardly believe this was a reality.

"I don't have a boyfriend, but I'm sure you know that, Jeff."

He looked down at her, his eyes wide with genuine surprise. "You don't?"

Mavis shook her head. "You didn't know that?"

Jeff shook his head and breathed an audible sigh of relief. "I, um, don't really keep up on those things, you know. I mean, I was hoping. Anyway, so what do you think? Do you want to hang out? I mean, *Star Child* is playing at the Eastwood... opening night. I know it's a Monday, but if we caught the first showing, we could be home by nine."

Mavis thought about it for a fraction of a second. Of course, she would go with him, but she didn't want to appear too eager. She had also taken subconscious notice of the fact that the halls were almost completely empty of students, and she didn't want to get a detention slip.

"Sure," she muttered.

A smile crossed Jeff's face, a real smile of happiness and relief. "Good." He started walking backward away from her. "So, I'll get you at six or so?"

Mavis nodded, still somewhat shocked, and offered him a slight smile in return. "Six. I'll be ready."

She ducked into her classroom, making it into her chair just as the bell rang. Had all of that really happened? Oh, my, Jeff Deason had just made a movie date with her! What if it was a setup? What if he didn't show, and all of his friends laughed their butts off?

But something told her that it wasn't a joke or a prank. Something inside of Mavis told her that the most popular boy in school, *Jeff Deason*, had just asked her out for a movie. Wow, wait until she told Kim!

Her mind was racing; didn't he have football practice after school? Yes, her head wanted to argue, but she made a firm decision right then and there that she wasn't going to argue with herself or overthink it. She would be ready for that date, and if he didn't show, she would proceed to embarrass him good for being a jerk.

Mavis recalled lying on the couch the night before,

thinking about this very moment and drumming it all up in her mind. She had thought about it and fantasized, and then Boom! Here it was. She didn't quite know what to think.

She wasn't ten minutes into class, or her dreamy state before her stomach started rumbling crazily. She was ravenous, and she had just eaten breakfast before school! It was enough to immediately take her mind off the pending date, and she mentally began counting the money in her purse. She would definitely be hitting up the vending machine, or she wouldn't make it through the day!

With that, she started to read, pushing Jeff Deason and chips out of her mind as best as she could.

∞

"I'm telling you, it's true!"

Kim and Mavis were walking home together, their arms bearing books. There had not been enough time in the second period for her to fill her best friend in on her surprise date request, so it had to wait until school was out. Kim had tried to bleed her for information, asking what Jeff had wanted and why he was at the locker, but Mavis had responded very nonchalantly. It would be fun to shock and surprise her best friend. Making the girl wait didn't matter to her; it was actually fun to speculate how her friend would react to the mind-blowing news.

But Kim's response was the complete opposite of what Mavis expected. She thought Kim would just die with surprise and envy. She even pictured the girl dropping her books all over the sidewalk, too shocked to carry them a step further.

"Okay," Kim finally conceded. "So, you are going to see *Star Child* with *Jeff Deason*, the Westside quarterback, tonight, when you have never had a date before. Just out of the blue he asks you out? Yeah, right. Sure, Mavis."

"Just out of the blue, I'm not kidding!"

At that point, the girl was finally convinced. She stopped right in the middle of the sidewalk, her mouth slightly agape and her eyes studying her best friend closely. Mavis stopped herself, and casually turned to her and waited patiently to hear whatever she was going to say. She couldn't believe her best friend thought she was making this all up! But, if she were honest, if Kim came to her with the same juicy tidbit, she wouldn't have completely believed it either; the two of them were not at the top of the 'Most Desired and Eligible Girls at Westside High' list after all.

"If what you are saying is true, and you have a real, true-to-life date with *Jeff Deason*—" she paused for effect, "I had better get an absolute full report, once you get back home and I mean right after you get home."

Mavis smirked. "Of course."

They started walking again. "So, what are you going to wear?" Kim asked.

Mavis shrugged. She hadn't thought about that yet at all. "I'm not sure."

Kim stopped again. "Wow! Do I have to hold your hand all the way to the theater too? I'm going to your house with you. This is definitely a job for me."

"I'll be fine, Kim," she replied. "It's a movie, so jeans and a t-shirt, I guess."

"Jeans and a t-shirt?!" Her friend looked as though she may have a heart attack. "No. No jeans, and no t-shirt. Hurry up." She started walking full speed ahead, leaving Mavis lagging behind. "If he's picking you up at six we have no time to lose."

They did not waste time. Kim went into Mavis' house with her, and, while she settled on a stylish pair of jeans, Kim chose a light blue sweater to go with it, claiming it would be casual, yet attractive.

"And it brings out your eyes."

Once she left, Mavis sat at her vanity looking at her reflection. She still looked the same; she hadn't blossomed into some kind of stunning beauty overnight or anything. So why had Jeff decided to just ask her out like that? It made absolutely no sense. Should she dare to think that he had been trying to work up the courage to ask her out for a while? That he, too, was shy and reserved just like her when it came to the opposite sex? She found it a little hard to believe.

Mavis studied her reflection a while longer; she supposed she did have nice eyes; they were blue, but her mother liked to say they were almost violet. Mavis also had very long, lush eyelashes, which were her own personal favorite feature. It was her hair that bothered her the most. It was long and mousy-brown, sort of. It curled on the ends, which was nice, but its flat color made her feel like an ugly stepsister in a world full of beautiful ones. Her stupid hair distracted the eye from her other, more appealing features, in her opinion.

When she was sick of staring at her own dumb face, she stood up and walked away. Her stomach was at it again, and if Jeff was picking her up at six, she had better eat something now. She went to the kitchen, scanned the fridge, and settled on a sandwich with the works; it took her ten minutes to build it. Topped off with chips (not the hot ones) and cold milk, it was almost the perfect snack. When it was finished, she stood back and got a good look at the plate. It was beautiful. If that didn't fill her stomach and get her through, nothing would.

By the time she was done eating it was four-thirty. Time to take a shower, and add some light makeup, and get dressed. Her parents would both be home by five-thirty, giving her just enough time to tell them about Jeff and the date. More importantly, she wanted to make sure to let them know to save her as much supper as possible. Jeff hadn't said a word about eating, and the way things had been going with her appetite, she would be more than ready to stuff her face by the time she got back home.

Considering what she had to work with, she had a lot to do and very little time to do it. Mavis quickly showered and dressed, then applied just a bit of blush and eye makeup, especially mascara, which was really all she ever felt she needed. She had never really been one for a lot of eyeliner, like some of the girls her age.

She combed her hair out and put it in rollers, then blow-dried it, and when she took the rollers out, it fell to her shoulders in long, soft curls. Mavis stared at her reflection for the second time that day. She had to admit, she looked good. Even a little… pretty.

"Mavis, we're home!"

Jane's voice echoed down the hall. Mavis grabbed her purse and cell, taking note of the time: five-thirty. Whoa, he would be here at six! Her stomach did a nervous flip, so she stopped and took a few deep breaths to calm her nerves.

At last, she left her room and went into the kitchen.

Jane turned to her. "Hi, hon… Well, will you look at this! You look beautiful, Mav! What's the occasion? An 'A' on that chlorophyll assignment?"

"Ha, ha," Mavis replied sarcastically. She opened the fridge and pulled out a piece of bologna, then rolled it into a tube and started to eat it; Jane watched her with wonder. "No. Actually, I have a… date."

"What?" Jane sat down hard at the table. "Sit, sit! A date? You're kidding me! With who? What's his name? What are you going to do? What's he like? Is he nice?"

"Mom, slow down." She joined her mother at the table and finished the rest of the cold cut. "It's Jeff Deason. He's on the football team, and he asked me to a movie tonight at six; right before first period today." Mavis smiled shyly. "He… he even walked me to class."

Todd came into the room at that moment. "What's all the racket in here?"

Jane looked up at her husband, beaming. "Our little Mav-Mav has a date!"

He stopped dead in his tracks, an open can of beer

frozen in place halfway to his mouth. "A date, huh? Really? Vroom, vroom!"

Mavis blushed a deep red. "Knock it off, you guys. I'm nervous enough, you know, and I could use some real support and advice."

"Just be yourself," they both declared in unison.

Mavis laughed out loud. "How did I know you were going to say that?" She looked at the kitchen clock nervously. "I just hope I'm capable of that. I feel like this is… sort of a big deal."

"I'd say!" Jane leaned forward and gave her daughter a long hug. "I'll be waiting up for you. It's a school night, so be home by ten. The film should be over in time if he's picking you up at six."

Mavis pulled away from her and went to check her appearance in the hall mirror. When she returned, they were both staring at her with goofy smiles on their faces. She loved them both so much.

With a bright smile, she told them, "Ten o'clock it is!"

CHAPTER 5

Star Child had been advertised as the hottest movie to hit theaters since the last sci-fi offering, and the world had been talking about it for weeks. Mavis wondered if they were going to get to the theater to discover that it was sold out, but Jeff managed to surprise her as soon as he arrived. He was just full of surprises, or so it seemed to Mavis.

For one thing, she honestly didn't even expect him to show at her house. But sure enough, at five minutes to six, there was a knock at the front door. Poor Mavis was pacing around like a crazy person, and when he knocked, she promptly jumped out of her skin.

She turned to her mother, panic all over her face. "I think I changed my mind."

But her mother wouldn't have it. Jane rose and answered the door, letting Jeff in and taking care of the introductions. Mavis' father gave him a nice, gentle grilling, mostly just because Jeff had a car and he wanted to be sure the young man would be driving responsibly with his daughter as a passenger. But with all that aside, things had gone smoothly.

On the way to his sports car, Mavis said, "I almost

didn't think you would really come."

Jeff laughed as he opened the passenger door for her. "Well, I had to duck out of football practice fifteen minutes early, but the coach doesn't give me much of a hassle." He looked her over, then hesitated before continuing. "Do you mean, you thought I was fooling around about this date?"

She nodded and settled into the seat, fastening her belt as he closed the door and walked around. He got in himself and buckled up, then sat there quietly for a minute. Mavis could tell he was giving her admission some thought. Finally, after a moment, he turned to her.

"You know, Mavis, I'm a pretty busy guy," he said. "Between football and class, and the fact that I have a part-time job on the weekends, my life is pretty full. To be honest, I don't get to go on dates as much as I would like. The truth is, I've noticed you, and I think you are pretty and smart. I'm glad you said yes."

She took a breath. "Thank you."

He turned the ignition on and continued. "By the way, I like your sweater. It makes your eyes look bright. You look really pretty, Mav. Can I call you 'Mav'?"

Blushing, she said, "Yes, everyone does. And thanks again."

They drove in silence for a very short time, then Mavis spoke up. "I guess since I've never had a date…"

She felt Jeff look over at her briefly. "It's okay; I'm not big on dating myself. I get really nervous around girls, usually. For instance, it took me almost three years to work up the nerve to talk to you." He gave her a smile and a wink. "Besides, we have to get to know each other to trust each other."

His words put Mavis at ease. Had he really been wanting to talk to her since junior high? Could he be telling the truth? She chose to believe him due to the trust statement he had made. Jeff was starting to seem like he had some integrity.

∞

Star Child turned out to be pretty good, contrary to what Mavis expected. It was about an alien whose sole purpose was to die to save the universe. It had good special effects and even sported a couple of scenes that brought a tear to her eye, which was a difficult feat. Overall, she enjoyed it, but more than anything she enjoyed the company she had.

Jeff turned out to be friendly, funny, and a perfect gentleman. About half-way through the movie, he reached over shyly to hold her hand; once she realized what he was doing, she let him. It was at that point, however, that she noticed the smell, and all the popcorn and candy in the world would not distract her from it.

First, it was just his aftershave. It was light and spicy and very pleasant. It also seemed to Mavis that she could smell his shampoo. But then she could smell his skin, and it was that aroma that started getting her going; when she got her first good whiff of it, she started to feel... hungry. He didn't just smell like pheromones or 'meat,' which she could also smell more keenly than usual. He smelled like steak, straight up. It was torture, and it seemed to be tearing at both her mind and stomach at the same time. Why did everything seem to smell so loud all of a sudden?

Mavis leaned over. "What is that you're wearing?"

Jeff smiled at her in the darkness. "It's called 'Sailboat' by O2," he whispered in her ear, causing her nose to go into overdrive. "My dad got it for me for my birthday last summer. Do you like it?"

Did she like it? It made him smell like a thousand medium-rare bacon cheeseburgers! Heck yes, she liked it! She loved it!

With a vigorous nod, she turned her attention back to the big screen. Jeff squeezed her hand gently and did the same. But Mavis soon realized she couldn't focus on the plot right then. She was subconsciously taking deep breaths and inhaling his essence, and her stomach was rumbling like thunder. Next, her mouth began watering so abundantly that she felt like one of those poor, starving children from television, who happened to be enduring somebody waving a steak under their nose, but keeping it just out of their reach.

It was torture, and before long she couldn't take a second more of it.

"Excuse me," she whispered into Jeff's ear. Without waiting for him to respond, Mavis rose and rushed out into the lobby, where she made her way directly to the food counter.

She briefly stood in line, hopping from one foot to the next as she decided what she wanted. When it was her turn, she said, "I'll take two hot dogs with everything, please."

The attendant quickly got the order together, and before long Mavis was standing next to a large pole scarfing down the hot dogs, juggling them as she did so. Mustard was on her upper lip, and a bit of relish was on her chin. She gulped the food down like a starving stray, wiped her mouth, and rushed back into the movie. How embarrassing that she had to binge-eat at the theater. What the heck was going on with her appetite, anyway?

Back inside, Jeff leaned over and asked, "Are you okay?"

She nodded. "Just needed to use the restroom. Sorry, it took so long; it was kind of packed."

The rest of the movie passed uneventfully, even though all she could smell was barbecued Jeff, so she pretty much missed the point of the film. At one point, Mavis even had to turn her head to dodge the smell. He must have eaten a darn good supper before he picked her up, maybe even cooked it himself. It had certainly seeped into his skin!

After the film, the pair took a roundabout way back to Mavis' house. They talked about school and football; they talked about Kim and Jeff's best friend Shawn. They also talked about what their parents did for a living. During the entire ride, Mavis had to keep her window partway down to air out the smell of the good-looking boy next to her.

At nine forty-five he pulled his car up in her driveway and shut off the ignition. Now came the awkward part of the first date that everyone dreaded. Would he try to kiss her? Should she linger just in case, or jump right out and say, 'See you tomorrow!' She didn't know, so she sat there, frozen and nervous.

"Hey! How about I walk you to your door," he suggested with an amused smile. "Isn't that the right way to do things?"

"Um, okay."

Jeff got out and walked around the car to let her out. He then followed her to the door, his pace deliberately slow. Mavis could tell he wanted to walk beside her, so she had to force herself to live with his wonderful scent. They stopped outside the door and turned to each other.

"Thanks for coming with me," Jeff said haltingly. "Um, I work Saturday morning, and I run some drills in the afternoon. If you're free Saturday evening we could, um, we could get something to eat at SportsBurger, or wherever you like... if you're free, that is."

"Sure," Mavis replied. "I'd like that."

Then, out of the blue, Jeff leaned over and kissed her. It was a soft, undemanding kiss that was no more than a smooch, but his lips lingered, and she got all rubbery at their soft touch. But then she smelled his skin again, and her stomach growled angrily. Jeff pulled back, a surprised, amused look on his face once again. She seemed to really entertain him, in one way or another.

"You're hungry!" he exclaimed with a smile as he pulled away. "You'd better go eat. On Saturday, I'll make sure you don't go through that at all, okay Mavis?"

She grinned and nodded, taking hold of the

doorknob nervously. "Okay, Jeff. Saturday. I'm looking forward to it. Oh, by the way, I had a great time."

Mavis tried to enter the house slowly, but her appetite was rushing her. It almost seemed that she couldn't even control herself. Had she actually been tempted to bite his lip when he kissed her? She could have sworn that the thought briefly crossed her mind! What the heck was going through her head?

She finally gave up on being gracious and rushed into her house, closing the door as he made his way to the car. She could hear him whistling lightly, and she felt bad that she had been so abrupt. Once inside, she quickly closed the door and leaned back against it, eyes closed and breathing heavily.

"Did you two save me any supper?" she yelled to her parents.

R.W.K. Clark

CHAPTER 6

At eleven o'clock that night, Mavis lay in bed with the blankets over her head and her cell phone pressed against her ear so her parents wouldn't hear her. She had already endured the third degree by her mother, who sat like a smiling vulture, listening to her recap as Mavis stuffed her face with deep-fried lobster bites, French fries, and stuffed mushrooms. Now she was on the phone with Kim, going through the entire 'third degree' thing for the second time. It was fun but was also exhausting.

"Mav," Kim, who had just answered on the first ring, said in greeting. "You are so lucky you called me; I wouldn't have been able to sleep a wink if you hadn't. So, fill me in! All details, Mav; *all* of them!"

They spent the next hour going through every single aspect of her date with Jeff, and Mavis left absolutely nothing out. Sure, she had agreed to fill in her best friend, but that wasn't why she was doing it. The real reason had to do with her appetite, and the fact that he smelled like prime beef, and the additional fact that she had been almost overwhelmingly tempted to bite his lip when he kissed her.

The first concern was her appetite. She told Kim about his aftershave, 'Sailboat,' and how good it smelled. Then she told her friend about how her stomach went crazy, and she had to sneak out of the movie just to shovel in a hot dog.

Kim paused at the revelation. "You did what?"

Mavis groaned. She knew how it sounded: about as rude and unladylike as one could possibly get. She tried to emphasize the fact that she thought she would die if she didn't get anything to eat right then, but Kim wasn't hearing it. Mavis went right from the hot dog story to the pair standing at the front door, the tentative date on Saturday, and the kiss they shared. In her personal opinion, changing the subject was the only way to end the nagging her friend was putting her through over the darn hot dogs.

When she told her about the kiss, and lightly mentioned wanting to bite Jeff's lip, Kim stopped her mid-sentence.

"Are you trying to tell me that when he kissed you, you wanted to bite him?" her friend asked. "What are you, some kind of weirdo? I never knew that about you. Wow, you have all kinds of secrets, don't you?"

Mavis closed her eyes and groaned to herself. "Yeah, that's what I'm saying, but no, I'm not a weirdo. I think I was just, I don't know, hungry. Ugh."

There was a long pause. "Mav, you know, you have been a bit weird lately. First the cookies and running home for lunch, after you already had breakfast. Then the hot dogs during the first date of your life ever, and now this biting thing. Do you feel okay, really?"

Mavis thought about it all, including coming home and demanding her supper. She had just been kissed for the first time, and it had followed her very first date, and that with the best-looking boy in school and all she had been able to think about was re-heated lobster rolls, limp fries, and slimy mushrooms?

"I feel fine, but it just seems like all I can think about is food," she groaned. "I don't understand it. To think of him as food is insane, I tell you!"

"Are you pregnant?" Kim asked her. "Maybe there is all kinds of stuff you're not telling me, Mavis Harvey."

Mavis gave a sarcastic laugh. "Oh, ha, ha. Right. Don't be weird, Kim."

"Well, it's not like it would hurt you to gain five pounds, Mav," her friend continued. "Anyway, make sure you do your homework; don't want date night interfering with your future, now, do you?"

"Already done. Did it at school."

Kim clucked her tongue. "Ugh. I'm so jealous. Everything comes easily to you; dates, homework, lobster bites. I'll talk to you tomorrow."

They said their goodbyes and Mavis snuggled under her comforter, her mind still stuck on Jeff and her stomach. Even now it growled, and she found her thoughts turning to the roasted or grilled scent of his flesh. How does a person smell like a full-blown meal, anyway?

After much tossing and turning, she finally fell

asleep, but that wasn't the end of her unrest. She ended up having a crazy dream, one that actually woke her up. A dream that was dreadfully real, and it managed to interrupt her ability to get good sleep for the rest of the night.

∞

Mavis was at Donnelly Park with her family, Kim's family, and the family of Jeff Deason. They were having a cookout, with all the dads gathered around the grill. Jeff, Mavis, and Kim were in the pool, splashing around and pushing each other in. It was a bright, sunny, warm day, and even within the confines of her dream, the water felt cool and refreshing.

Suddenly, Mavis heard her father yell, 'Come and get it!' She looked around for her friends, but she could just find Kim. "Where did Jeff go?" she asked her friend.

"He was due for lunch," Kim replied.

The girls made their way to their families, all of whom were seated at picnic benches. Before them were plates covered with sterling silver domes, like rich people used, and no one else at the table had started eating yet. There were even candles lit on the picnic table, which Mavis vaguely thought was weird, considering they were all outside at a park in the middle of the day.

Their family members were all seated, but they all turned around and looking for the girls. Mavis noticed right away that Jeff didn't seem to be among them, and she asked Kim once again, "I wonder where Jeff is?" Kim simply repeated her earlier statement, which Mavis found frustrating. He wasn't even at the table! What did she mean, 'he was due for lunch?' She was just goofy.

When they reached the table they found they were seated right next to each other; their covered plates were waiting for them. When they sat down, Kim eagerly removed the cover from her plate to reveal barbecued chicken, a pile of pasta salad, and a smaller pile of baked beans. It looked wonderful. She turned to Mavis with a smile.

"Mmm, mmm, good!" she said with a smile.

Next, Mavis reached for the handle of her cover. She hesitated and looked up and down the table; everyone's food looked so delicious! She could smell each and every item, from the chicken to the pasta salad, and drool was running down her chin. Finally, she couldn't wait anymore, and she lifted the cover from her plate.

Suddenly, Mavis let out a blood-curdling scream.

Jeff's head was on her plate, looking up at her with a big grin. His long, blond hair was arranged perfectly around the area where his neck used to be, and it was surrounded by big lettuce leaves and a couple of cherry tomatoes. His blue eyes were sparkling, and he seemed fairly cheerful.

"Looks pretty tasty, huh, Mav?" he asked her. "Don't need no sauce for this dish; it's nice, fresh, and juicy-juicy too!"

He paused and looked around at the lettuce. "You might want a little dressing for that, though!"

Jeff began to laugh.

She tried to tell Kim and everyone else what they had served her; it had to be a mistake! But no one would listen, and soon, the smell of him overwhelmed her. She picked his head up like a basketball and sank her teeth into his cheek.

"That's right, Mav!" he exclaimed cheerfully. "Dig in, girl! Fresh meat! Fresh meat! All you need is fresh meat!"

∞

She jerked awake, covered in sweat, her hair wet and matted to her skull. What in the world was that?! That had to be the craziest thing she had ever dreamed.

But her thoughts were soon drowned out by her growling tummy, and Mavis flung her feet to the floor with a sigh.

"Might as well eat since I'm awake," she mumbled as she patted her tummy on her way to the kitchen.

CHAPTER 7

"So, Mavis, you have to fill in your father on the date," Jane said, scooping the second pile of hash browns onto her daughter's plate; Todd was just staring at his daughter. She was shoveling food in like a madwoman, and it was obvious by the look on his face that he was a bit taken aback by it all.

Mavis was scooping bite after bite into her mouth; it was her second full plateful of food, and she had to leave for school in fifteen minutes.

Both her mother and father squinted at her as if they couldn't believe their eyes. "What?" they both said in unison.

Mavis finished chewing, took a drink of milk, and said, "It was good. Just a movie, you know."

Jane leaned forward conspiratorially. "Tell your father about the kiss and the date on Saturday!"

"Mom!" Mavis noticed right away that Todd looked like he was having a stroke. She took a deep breath. "Just a nice, friendly kiss. A fast one, Dad, so don't worry."

She flashed her mother a look that the woman immediately understood, then went back to her food.

Mavis all but inhaled the second helping before draining her milk glass and putting her dishes in the sink. Her mother always made her so nervous, acting like they were best friends and all. Even though they were close, she didn't have to put her on the spot while her dad was sitting there.

"Are you anxious to see him again?" Jane asked, a sly grin on her face.

Mavis grabbed her books and nodded. "Saturday. Look, I have to go, or I'm going to be late."

She quickly gave them both a peck on the cheek and headed out the door. She couldn't wait to see Kim; she wanted to tell her about her dream. Mavis also figured she might mention that she woke from it feeling like she hadn't eaten in a month. She was starting to think that maybe she needed to see the doctor.

Kim was just coming up the sidewalk when Mavis stepped outside, so they joined up without hesitation and started for school. During their walk, Mavis told her about the dream, and just as she suspected, Kim told her to make a doctor appointment, or at least tell her mother. It didn't sound right, especially for Mavis, to have an insatiable appetite constantly. She might have some kind of deficiency somewhere.

"So, did you get along?" Kim asked her as they climbed the steps to the high school building. "Are you going to see him again, do you think?"

"Saturday, Kim. I told you that last night." She was getting frustrated with everyone.

Her friend stopped right in her tracks and turned to

her. "Are you copping an attitude with me?"

Mavis turned to her. "No. I'm sorry. I guess I just had to listen to my mother and father, both last night and this morning, digging for information, too. Just got a little frustrated, that's all."

Kim studied her face, and then the two started walking again, taking the first right in the hall to go to Mavis' locker. "I wasn't trying to make you mad. Just excited that one of us finally got a date, Mav, and not just any date. A date with the elite, the most popular boy in school, you know?"

Mavis didn't even bother to answer. The fact was that Kim was right; there was no way out of talking about any time she spent with Jeff. Everyone in her world would want every single last morbid detail, no matter what. It was all because dates just weren't something she, or her best friend, were asked on. At their age, getting dates was expected.

∞

While she dug through her locker and chose the right textbooks for her classes, Kim rambled on about an argument she had with her older brother, the night before. According to her, he had snuck into her room and borrowed her very fancy and very expensive earbuds without her permission. When she couldn't find them, she went into his room to discover them submerged in an old, half-moldy glass of orange juice. Needless to say, she had blown a fuse. Kenny had gotten grounded, plus lost his allowance for the next month in order to replace the pair. Her parents really hit him where it hurt.

As Mavis closed her locker and the girls walked away to head for class, a boy ran by them full speed ahead down the hall. He was running so fast that his book bag, which he was holding out behind him, caused a breeze. Enough of a breeze, in fact, that it blew the girls' hair slightly.

That was when Mavis caught the smell of bacon; it was coming off of Kim in waves. Her belly started tormenting her right away. She glanced at her friend, who was shaking her head now and complaining about the careless young hallway runner.

"Did you have bacon for breakfast?" Mavis interrupted.

Kim gave her an odd look. "Uh, no. I told you I had Cinnamon Crisps, remember?"

Mavis thought about it as they climbed the stairs. "Yeah, I guess. But did your mom make bacon? Because you smell like yummy bacon."

"There was no bacon, Mav."

At the upper landing, she leaned over and took a big sniff of her friend. "Yep," she said. "Big-time bacon."

"I didn't have bacon, Mavis," Kim replied in a grumbly voice. "And I showered this morning. Everything is food with you, I swear. I'll see you in science."

With that, Kim walked away, her left hand pulling her hair to her face and smelling it. Mavis shrugged. She didn't mean to make her best friend mad, but she did smell like bacon, just like Jeff smelled like steak. With a quick look around, she saw that the hall was clearing, and she began to lightly jog to get to her Lit class on time.

But as it turned out, her two friends' meat-like aromas were just the beginning. She had no more settled into her desk and opened her copy of *Passage of Time* than Mavis was overwhelmed with powerful smells. From pork chops to bologna, all she could smell was meat, in one form or another, and she couldn't concentrate on the pages before her than a dog could chase a ball with a bone lying right in front of his face.

Mavis began to squirm. She was looking at her neighboring students out of the corner of her eyes. Had everyone brought their lunch in with them? Her stomach began to painfully demand satisfaction; what time was it? One look at the clock told her it was only eight fourteen; the bell would ring in less than a minute.

She didn't think she was going to make it until lunch.

Her book was completely forgotten before she even started to read. Mavis began to actually sweat; in her peripheral vision, she saw that one boy sitting to her right actually had his sack lunch under his seat, along with, what appeared to be all his school books. He must have been late and not had time to stop at his locker.

She almost felt like she immediately lost all sanity. Mavis looked up at Miss Hawkins' desk; the woman sat there making marks in her big, grade book. Next, Mavis glanced around the room; it seemed like everyone was oblivious to everyone else. Perfect!

Leaning over, she whispered to the boy, whose name was Tommy Johnson, "Hey, Tommy! Can I buy that lunch from you?"

In a painfully slow manner, the kid turned his head and looked at her in disbelief. After a moment, he silently mouthed, "What?"

"Your lunch," she repeated. "I want to buy your lunch."

He gave her a confused, shrug. "What'll I eat then?"

"I'll pay you! Whatever you want!" Mavis fished some folded money from her hip pocket and flashed it at him. "I've got cash!"

Miss Hawkins broke in sternly. "Miss Harvey! Mr. Johnson! Eyes on books!"

Both of them immediately pulled themselves apart and looked back down at their assigned reading. After a moment, though, the smells took hold of her again. She looked back at Tommy Johnson and his lunch.

"Ten bucks," she whispered. "I'll give you ten bucks."

"Miss Harvey!" Now Miss Hawkins rose and made her way up the aisle between Mavis and Tommy. "What seems to be the issue?"

Tommy began to tremble. He was also known for stuttering when he was nervous, and he definitely didn't disappoint in that department, either. Mavis felt bad for him, but hardly. She could barely cope with the scents that were taking over her sanity.

"M-M-Miss H-Hawkins," he began. "M-M-Mavis j-just wanted t-to know if sh-sh-she could b-b-buy my lunch."

The teacher looked at her, a look of frustration and disgust on her face. "You want to buy his lunch? Didn't you eat this morning, Miss Harvey?"

Mavis nodded.

"This isn't like you, Mavis," she continued. "Now, I won't have you disrupting the class. Visit the vending machines between classes, but I don't want to hear another peep from either of you. Do you understand?"

Miss Hawkins went back to her desk, and both Mavis and Tommy put their eyes on their books. But it didn't matter; poor Mavis couldn't control the urges and drives she felt. She was shaking terribly, and her mouth was salivating so much she had to clamp her lips together to keep the spit in her mouth.

But then, everything took a turn for the worse.

It was as though a gray mist started to fill her vision, beginning at its very edges. Her palms got all sweaty, but she felt cold to the bone. Mavis didn't even have to think it through; she was incapable of thinking it through. She reached over, grabbed the lunch from the metal book basket under Tommy's seat, and she ran out of the class, laughing loudly and leaving her possessions behind.

Halfway down the stairs, she heard Miss Hawkins yell, "Mavis Harvey, you get back here right this minute!"

She ignored the call and ran all the way to the first-floor girls' room. Locking herself in the last stall, she tore into the lunch sack, eager and practically foaming at the mouth. Mavis looked like a drug addict about to indulge in a much-needed fix.

But then, she stopped dead in her tracks; it was peanut butter and jelly, carrots, chips, and a dollar bill.

It was too late for regret now. She began to inhale the food, smacking her lips and dropping bits to the floor as she stuffed it into her mouth. Literature and Miss Hawkins were forgotten; she was feasting! So distracted was she, that she didn't even hear the bathroom door open, or the footsteps approaching her stall.

"Miss Harvey, I'm going to need you to come out of there immediately!" It was Miss Hawkins.

Stunned back to reality, Mavis dropped the food to the floor and focused on the shoes on the other side: a pair of black women's flats, and a pair of men's penny loafers. Miss Hawkins had Mr. Pearson, the principal, with her.

Reaching up, Mavis slid back the bolt on the stall door and let it swing open. The two educators stared at her PB & J covered chin, glancing at the mess on the floor as well. They both shook their heads in unison.

"Miss Harvey," Mr. Pearson said sternly, "I'm afraid you are going to have to come with me."

CHAPTER 8

"Marsha Thomas?"

Mavis glanced up at the receptionist, who stood with a clipboard calling for Dr. Meadows' next patient. Turning her attention back to her fidgeting hands in her lap, she braced herself. Brief interruption aside, her mother was sure to start lecturing her again.

"I just don't understand it," Jane continued in a hushed tone, as if on cue. "Your father won't either, you know. Say something, Mavis! Explain to me how you could steal a boy's lunch! What is going on with you?"

Mavis groaned. "I don't know," she whispered back. "I was just so hungry…"

"I made you biscuits and gravy this morning!" her mom exclaimed, and not so quietly this time. "I had to get up early to do it, and you had two-and-a-half freaking servings! You act like you are neglected and abused or something! Stealing a sack lunch?"

Mavis maintained a whisper, hoping her mother would revert to one herself. "I offered him ten dollars for it."

"You had just eaten less than an hour before!" Now whispering, because there were other patients in the waiting room starting to stare, their magazines open on their laps. "You are grounded, and in so much trouble, Mavis."

All she could do was a sigh. "Mom, please. Wait 'til we leave, then tear into me, okay? I don't know why; it was like I... like I wasn't myself."

Jane went quiet then as if thinking about what her daughter said. They both remained still for the next ten minutes, the topic dropped for the time being. Mavis didn't even care about the consequence, as long as her mother let it go right at that moment.

Regardless, her mind was flooded. All she could smell, even there in Dr. Meadows' office, was meat. She felt weak with hunger, and couldn't wait to go home and have lunch. Should she tell the doctor about all the meat smells? Was that perhaps a sign of some sickness she didn't know about?

"Mavis Harvey?"

Both she and her mother stood at once, Jane taking hold of her daughter's arm as if she believed that Mavis might freak out and try to run. They both smiled at the receptionist and followed her back into an exam room. Soon, they were both seated, with Mavis enduring the typical blood pressure and temperature tests.

Dr. Meadows' nurse finished with those tasks and then sat, her pen poised to take notes. She began to ask questions regarding why they decided to visit that day. Jane began to let her words pour out, so Mavis kept her trap shut.

After Jane had managed to vent her emotions to the

nurse sufficiently, the woman said, "Okay. That's helpful. Now, Mavis, why don't you tell me what's going on with you."

Mavis glanced at her mom, who was sitting there with crossed arms and pursed lips, waiting to hear what kind of creative bullcrap Mavis came up with.

"I'm super-hungry, like, all the time," she began.

The nurse nodded and smiled at her condescendingly as she typed on the computer.

"Um, everyone smells like… meat."

Now the nurse stopped typing, almost freezing in her place. She shifted her eyes toward Mavis, then back to Jane before recovering her lost smile and responding. She even turned to Mavis as if to give the girl her full attention.

"Did you say, meat?"

Mavis nodded; Miranda Cassel's fingers resumed their typing.

"Other symptoms besides the… the smell of meat?"

Mavis shrugged. "Well, like my mother sort of said, I'm hungry all the time. I mean, even right after I eat, and I can eat really big meals. Like, this morning, I had more than two platefuls of biscuits and gravy, then I… well, I…"

"She went to school and stole some poor boy's peanut butter and jelly sandwich," my mother exclaimed. "We feed her; I promise, we feed her well. She has never eaten like this before in her life. As a matter of fact, getting her to clean her plate was always a struggle. But now, well, I don't think there is enough food in existence!"

Nurse Miranda gave a surprised look to Mavis. "You stole his lunch?"

She shrugged, embarrassed. "It was like I didn't know what I was doing. Besides, it smelled like leftover pot roast."

"Pot roast?" Jane and Miranda both exclaimed at once.

"Pot roast." Mavis gave a long, ragged sigh and lay down on the exam table, completely beside herself that she was such a spectacle at the moment.

Miranda was typing furiously now, and her brow was knitted with concern. The truth was that Mavis had been Dr. Meadows' patient most of her life. He and his office staff knew her well. It was not in her nature to steal, and it definitely wasn't in her nature to eat the way she was eating.

The nurse typed furiously on her keyboard briefly for a final time, then stood, offering both Mavis and her mother an obligatory smile. "Dr. Meadows will be right with you."

When she was gone, Mavis looked over at her mother. "I understand you are upset with me over Tommy's lunch, but we both know it's not like me to do things like that. You're acting like I'm some kind of incorrigible child who has a long history of acting like a criminal."

Jane closed her eyes and sighed. "Yes. Fine. I'm sorry I have overreacted. But whatever the doctor says, we do. If he says medicine, blood work, or even go straight to bed for six months, you will cooperate. Do you understand?"

Mavis barely had time to nod in agreement before a light knock came at the exam room door and Dr. Meadows walked in.

"Mavis!" he greeted. "So, you've been feeling a bit out of sorts, I hear."

She nodded yet again, and for the next ten minutes they discussed the issue once again, but this time Jane was not allowed to speak. Dr. Meadows believed that Mavis was old enough to speak for herself regarding her symptoms, and her mother's constant interjections were nothing more than an annoyance.

When they were finished, he said, "Okay, so here is what I want to do. Before you leave today I am going to have Miranda take some blood for us to check; we have to make sure that you don't have some kind of virus or bacterial infection that is causing this immense appetite of yours. Second, you have no fever or other symptoms that would imply illness, and you definitely don't have a weight problem, so if you are hungry, well, eat! Sometimes, if we smell or crave specific food types it means that we are deficient a specific nutrient; with meat, you could be lacking iron. We'll check that with the blood work as well. In the meantime, if you want meat, eat it. If you are hungry all the time, eat. We'll call you if there are any abnormalities, but otherwise, I think this may just be a growth spurt or a passing phase."

Both Mavis and her mother agreed, and the doctor bade them farewell and left.

About five minutes later she gave up a few tubes of her blood, then she and her mother left for home. On the way, Mavis asked for a burger and fries, and they went through the SportsBurger drive-thru. She tore into the food like she'd been starved, and Jane watched her out of the corner of her eye, cringing the entire time.

Mavis didn't care; that burger tasted like a prime rib sandwich, but she wished it had come to her a bit more on the rare side.

CHAPTER 9

Mavis spent the rest of her day trying to dodge concerned looks and forget the long lectures she endured. By the time she and Jane returned home from Dr. Meadows' office it was nearly noon, and even though she had eaten her burger and fries, the first thing she asked her mother was, 'What's for lunch?"

They had just walked in; as a matter of fact, Jane hadn't even put her jacket in the closet, and her purse still hung from her shoulder. She looked at her daughter in disbelief, mouth agape and eyes wide. Mavis simply waited for her response patiently as she hung her own jacket up.

"Did you just ask what we were eating for lunch?" her mother replied. "Burgers and fries. I would think you would remember; you just had lunch."

"That was lunch?"

Jane's shoulders sagged in defeat. "I'll have to look."

"Well, I'm going to text Kim and ask her to go to my teachers for my assignments. Let me know when it's ready."

Jane watched her daughter go to her room, shook her head, and made her way to the kitchen. She was concerned, that much was true. Even though the appetite thing would turn out to be good (Mavis was something of a scarecrow) Jane just couldn't get past the fact that her beloved, well-grounded daughter had snatched some poor kid's sack lunch and run to the bathroom. She was thoroughly embarrassed that the principal and Literature teacher discovered her shoveling it in, her face smeared with the sandwich fillings. It was almost as if Mavis was on drugs.

Yes! That was it! That explained the insane cravings and constant hunger. That also explained the lack of moral decision-making skills she was displaying. Just wait until Todd found out about the lunch, and the subsequent two-day suspension Mavis received as a result of the theft.

Jane put water on to boil, her foot tapping the floor at full speed. She would make macaroni and cheese with sliced hot dogs in it. That was what Mavis would get until supper, and that was it. She had better accept it.

She went to her daughter's room and knocked on the door. "Mavis, we need to talk."

"Come in."

Jane opened the door; Mavis sat in the middle of her bed, her cell lying in front of her, and a copy of *Supreme Chef* open to slices of medium-rare beef drizzled with some kind of dark sauce. The girl's mouth was open, and her tongue was hanging out slightly. She didn't even look up from the colorful photo spread before her.

"Did you text Kim for your homework?" Jane asked.

Mavis nodded her head and turned the page of the magazine, revealing grilled pork steaks with corn on the cob. It appeared to the woman that the food magazine was acting as something of an explicit nature, the way Mavis was acting. She was now licking her lips freely.

"Did she answer?"

At last her daughter looked up at her, briefly. "No, but she'll see it, and she'll do it. I've done it for her a million times, Mother." She turned another page.

"Are you on drugs, Mavis?"

Now she had Mavis' attention in full. The girl swung her head in her mother's direction, a look of sheer shock and surprise on her face. Had her mom really just asked her such a thing?

"Drugs? Wha—no! Of course, not! You know better than that!" She closed the magazine dramatically and jumped up off the bed. "You know that my grades are top-notch. I never spend any extra money, other than what I tell you about. How can you ask me that?"

Jane shrugged. "Then you won't mind taking a urine test for me. I'll go get one from Super Value Mart while you eat your lunch."

Immediately, Jane's question, as well as the impending drug test, were forgotten. "What did you make me for lunch?"

"Aargh!" Jane turned on her heel and left the room, slamming the door behind her.

Oh, well, Mavis thought. Drug test, shrug mess, she'd give a stupid pee sample. No problem. Mavis put the threatened test out of her mind and hoped her mother wasn't warming up Hamburger leftovers again. Another round in the oven and its new name would be 'Sand-burger Helper.'

Her cell phone rang, and she looked at it to see that Kim was calling. "Hello?"

"I'm in the girls' room, and I don't have much time," her friend said. "Why do I need to pick up your homework?"

Mavis groaned loudly. "It's a long story, and we don't have time to go into it now. Just stop by on your way home, okay?"

"Mavis, the food is done!"

"I have to go, Kim," she grumbled. "My mom's on a rampage; she thinks I'm on drugs. I'll see you after school."

Without waiting for a response, she hung up the phone and rushed out to the kitchen, where Jane was putting her jacket back on.

"Your food is on the table," she told her daughter sternly. "I'm going to buy that test. Don't leave the house; I'll be home shortly."

Soon, her mother was gone, and Mavis looked over at the plate of mac and cheese. She glanced back at the front door; the coast was clear. Opening the refrigerator, Mavis' eyes fell immediately on a package wrapped in white freezer paper. She picked it up and read the sticker: pork chops. A quick squeeze told her they were completely thawed out.

Giving no second thought to what she was about to do, Mavis unwrapped the package and took a single chop from it. She held it to her nose and inhaled deeply. Oh, my, it smelled like Junie Ryan, the girl who sat behind her. She hurried and re-wrapped the rest of the chops, then fetched the Scotch tape out of the nearby junk drawer and fastened the whole thing neatly back together and returned it to its plate on the shelf in the fridge.

Sitting down, chop in hand, she lifted a single slice of bread and slapped the small slab down on the sandwich. Looking at it, she considered the bone, then grabbed a steak knife and cut the meat away and put the bone aside. In seconds, she was tearing into the sandwich, grunts, and groans escaping her lips. A trickle of spit tinged with blood dripped down her chin, so she caught it with her finger and licked it clean.

When Mavis was finished eating she rinsed off her dishes, offered a massive belch, and wrapped her bone in plastic. It would make a great late-night snack, provided her mother didn't catch her with it.

∞

"Okay, this is how we are going to deal with this."

Todd was sitting in the living room with his wife and daughter after returning home from work early that evening. Mavis had already gone through a major confrontation regarding a missing pork chop, but her squeaky-clean urine test bought her way out of that one. Now, they all sat in a family meeting, and both Jane and Mavis had just wrapped up telling her father about the stolen lunch and doctor appointment.

"I'm not going to ground you," he continued. "But

the one reason is that Dr. Meadows seems to think you have a deficiency." His office had, indeed, called, and informed Jane that Mavis was extremely anemic, with such a low iron level that they were surprised the young high-schooler had any energy at all. "But, you will write a letter of apology to this young man, and you will give him ten dollars of your own money. In the future, I suggest you start packing some kind of snacks in your bag to have in class. Your mother will write a note about your anemia so you won't get into trouble for it; she'll also be picking up some supplemental iron tablets for you tomorrow, which you will take every day."

Mavis was eager to eat and go to her room. Kim had brought her assignments, just as she promised, and she had prodded Mavis for all the details about her day. As would be expected, the girl left stunned that her friend stole someone's lunch and had to be pursued by school authorities. The two agreed they would talk on the phone later.

Supper went quickly; even though she had two pork chops (which she thought were overcooked, since they were so dry) and three helpings of potatoes and corn. Even though they tried to make it not so obvious, Mavis could feel her parents' concerned eyes on her throughout the meal. By the time she excused herself and rinsed her dishes, she couldn't get out of their presence fast enough. She knew they were concerned, but aside from her insatiable hunger, she felt fine; that's what they should be going by.

Flopping down hard on her bed, she grabbed her

cell off the nightstand and dialed Kim.

"So, are you grounded?" her best friend greeted.

"Ugh," she replied. "No; the doctor says I'm anemic, and it probably made me do it. I have to take an iron pill and stuff. Anyway, since I have a two-day suspension, I'm sure I'll be better by the time I return on Friday."

Kim cleared her throat. "Jeff asked about you today after I left your house, by the way."

Mavis sat up straight in her bed. "He did? What did he say?"

"Oh, not much. He said he heard about Tommy Johnson's lunch. He said he heard that you barricaded yourself in the bathroom, and they had to break the door down to get you out."

"That's a lie!" Mavis yelled. "OMG, I'm going to die!"

Her friend laughed. "Don't worry, psycho. I straightened him out. Actually, he thought the whole thing was a riot, and he told me he thinks you're one of the coolest girls he ever met. He really likes you, Mav."

She laid back again, her mind still racing. "So, what did you tell him?"

"I just said the lunch thing was a joke, and you got two days in jail," she replied with a snicker. "I wouldn't worry; he thought it was funny and cool. He said he wanted to call you, so I made sure he had your number."

Mavis groaned inwardly; he was going to call her? Oh, she didn't know what to say to him. Well, too late to worry about that now.

"Okay, Kim. I have to get off the phone and hit the books. Call me tomorrow?" They hung up, for as long as they had known each other, if either of them missed school for any reason, the other would fill them in on any gossip or excitement that might arise.

Mavis stood to grab her books from her desk; she liked to study on her bed, and the desk was nothing more than a catch-all and vanity. Laptop and books in hand, she plopped down, propped her pillows behind her back, and set about studying.

But immediate studious behavior was not to be. Her phone rang, and when she didn't recognize the number on display, she knew it was Jeff. She held the phone, staring at the screen, and took some deep breaths.

"Hello?"

There was a pause. "Mavis? It's Jeff."

Leaning back, she closed her eyes. She wanted to sound cool and collected, but she didn't feel that way. Trying to relax, she answered him.

"Yeah, Jeff. It's me. What's up?"

Another pause. "Um, I hope you don't mind; I got your number from your friend Kim."

"She told me," Mavis replied, forcing her best cheerful voice. "No problem."

He coughed, then cleared his throat. "So, are you okay? Crazy day at school, huh?"

She laughed as though it was nothing. "Yeah. Just had the urge to break the monotony, I guess."

He laughed as well. "Well, you're kind of the talk of

the school. I don't think anyone knew you had it in you. Heck, I have guys on the football team who think you're like… awesome. Crazy!"

They both laughed again until it petered out. Mavis could hear his breathing, and it seemed rapid and ragged. Was he okay?

"Jeff? Are you okay?"

"Oh!" he said suddenly. "Oh, yeah. Listen, Mavis, I know we have a date Saturday evening."

Mavis heart immediately froze in her chest. Was he going to cancel? Did the stunt she pulled with Tommy's lunch freak him out more than he was willing to admit?

He continued. "But I was wondering, you know if it goes okay, would you go with me to homecoming?"

She didn't even think about it; the words flew from her mouth without any thought whatsoever. "Sure! Of course! I'd love to!"

Mavis could literally hear his relief over the phone, and she wondered if the disbelief she felt at his asking was as audible. She sat quietly, waiting for him to speak. Suddenly, the aroma of raw meat hit her nose hard, and Jeff was forgotten for a second. Was that supper cooking? What was that smell? Her belly did a violent flop of longing.

"Awesome," Jeff said. "So, I guess I'll see you at the school Friday. Can I call you before then?"

Mavis was walking around now, looking for the source of the meat smell. "Sure, yes. Any time."

To her relief, they said their goodbyes. She tossed her phone onto the bed and crept out into the hall, then snuck to the kitchen door. Mavis could smell the lingering scent of dinner, but the raw meat aroma was gone. She stood there in the darkness of the hall, confused. Then it hit her: her bone!

She ran back to her room and got into her closet, retrieving the plastic-wrapped pork chop bone from its hiding place: one of last year's sneakers. In seconds, Mavis had it unwrapped, and she stood with her back to her bedroom door, gazing out the window into the twilight, as she gnawed on it like a dog, scraping with her teeth for any meaty remnants she could get.

"What are you doing?"

She spun around, surprised at her mother's voice. The blood-tinged pork chop bone hung from her teeth, but she was so taken off-guard that she didn't even think about it. Her mother gaped at her in horror.

"What?" Mavis asked her.

"Is that a pork chop bone?" Jane asked with shock. She walked slowly to her daughter, her eyes glued to the bone. "Mavis, that's a raw bone! Is that from my missing chop? Did you eat a raw pork chop?"

Mavis slowly removed the bone from her mouth, oblivious to the pink smear of blood on her lips and chin. She smiled and shrugged, embarrassed. Her mother looked both horrified and furious.

"Um, yeah?"

As Jane grabbed her daughter by the collar of her shirt, the bone went flying from her hand, hitting the wall and dropping to the floor. Jane said nothing; she simply dragged the girl down the hall and into the living room, where Todd was reclined in his chair watching some comedy and laughing like a hyena.

"Todd!" Jane now had a grip on Mavis' arm that threatened to break it if the girl tried to jerk away.

The man jumped and turned to them. "What?"

"I just caught your daughter eating a raw pork chop bone!" Jane gave the girl's arm a jerk. "My missing chop bone, at that!"

Within a half-hour, the three of them were seated in the waiting room of the ER at Grace Mercy Hospital, her mother crying and her father pissed that he was missing his show. They wanted to be sure the raw pork wouldn't hurt her, but that wasn't all. They took Mavis there to see an emergency shrink.

Oh, well, she thought as she thumbed through a worn copy of 'Food Envy.' Maybe they'll stop for burgers on the way home.

R.W.K. Clark

CHAPTER 10

Mavis woke to the sunlight streaming through her window and hitting her in the face. She lay with her eyes closed, just enjoying its warmth, for several minutes. Finally, her hunger drove her to get out of her cozy cocoon and start her day. A glance at the clock told her it was nearly ten in the morning, and the fact made her smile; she didn't even sleep this late on the weekends.

It didn't feel like a Wednesday, because they had been at the ER until nearly midnight threw her off a bit, she knew. She smiled as she dressed, recalling the doctors the night before. They thought her health would be fine; if she got sick her parents could bring her back, but it would likely run its course.

The shrink had leaned heavily on Dr. Meadows' diagnosis, even saying that her severe anemia may have thrown off her judgment. He insisted on iron, gave her mother some medicine to relax, and sent them all home. But not before he showered Mavis with plenty of strange skeptical looks. She didn't think he even believed his own words about the effects of the anemia, but she was obviously sane. She didn't think it was so weird at all; some people loved raw pork, didn't they?

Shrugging it off, she dressed and made her way to the kitchen to eat. Food was the first thing on her mind, once she put the hospital visit memory where it belonged. She didn't even bother to brush her hair or anything, she just wanted to eat. Mavis wondered what her mother made for breakfast as she hummed her way down the hall.

Jane was at the table going through bills. She gave Mavis a glance, then did a double-take. Concern was all over her face.

"Mavis, you're white as a ghost!"

Her mom's words almost didn't register. "What?" she asked as she turned to look in the hall mirror.

Her own appearance almost bowled her over. Her skin was pasty white, almost albino-like. Her eyes were rimmed with red, and her hair was a mess. The fact was she looked like death.

"Yes, this is Jane Harvey. I was in yesterday with my daughter Mavis." Her mother was on the phone, and Mavis knew she was calling Dr. Meadows; at this point, she didn't blame her. "She is white as a ghost! I picked up her iron, and we even saw the ER doctor last night, and he said it was low iron, but I mean, she looks dead!"

Mavis stood at the kitchen door, watching her mother and eyeballing the fridge. Was it the wrong time to rummage? Maybe she should find the iron pills her mom said she bought and take one. Right away she took notice of a paper bag with "Dale's Pharmacy" printed on it, so she opened it, pulled the iron pills out, and dug in, taking the first one she got her fingers on.

"Yes, she just took one," her mother was saying as she stared, horrified, at her daughter. "Okay. Okay, I'll do that. Thank you." Jane turned to her daughter. "You make sure to take that every single morning; I'll be sure to have one at your plate for breakfast. Now, what do you want to eat? Dr. Meadows said you need lots of red meat, lots of stuff high in iron."

Mavis shrugged. "Whatever you want to make me, Mom; I'm starving." She plopped down hard in her chair. "Just so you know, I feel great. I mean, I never felt better, really!"

Jane pulled some sausage out of the refrigerator and plopped the package on the counter, then removed some frozen meat from the freezer to thaw. "Liver it is," she averred firmly, giving Mavis a look of doubt at her last statement. "And on the side, you can have both kale and spinach."

Mavis crumpled her nose and stuck out her tongue. "Kale and spinach? Mom!"

Jane stopped egg carton in hand and confusion on her face. "The liver doesn't upset you? You have always despised liver, Mav!"

The girl sat back and knit her brow as she thought. She had always hated liver, but now it really sounded juicy and yummy. "Can you cook it, so it's a little, you know, pink in the middle?"

"No!"

Mavis groaned. "Fine, all right. So, what are you making for breakfast?"

"Well," Jane replied, "I had bran flakes, which are

iron-fortified if you'd like that, But otherwise, I can cook you some eggs, sausage, and toast, which…" she cringed. "Which should be fine since you took some iron. But starting with lunch, you are going to be eating differently. My, you have no color at all! And your eyes! They're all rimmed with red. I don't know what to think, Mavis. You are going to be the death of me. I'm putting some spinach in your eggs and you young lady are having an omelet. I'm going to the store when I'm done to stock up."

While her mother pulled out her frying pan and a bag of leaf spinach, Mavis pretended to gag, but she kept quiet about it. "So, I talked to Jeff last night, Mom. He asked me to homecoming."

Her mother whirled around and nearly dropped her spatula. "He did? Oh, my, he did?"

The woman put her spatula down without a second thought and rushed to the table. Grabbing Mavis by the hands, she pulled her to her feet, and together, right there in the kitchen, the mother and daughter danced in circles, hand in hand, anemia and stolen pork chops forgotten and far behind them.

When they stopped, Jane pulled Mavis to her and hugged her tightly. "I knew this would happen for you, Mav. You're so pretty and so smart and funny. I just knew it, and a football player, too? Oh, wait until your dad hears!"

Mavis had a smile plastered to her face; her mother was genuinely happy for her, and regardless of all the parental nagging and complaining she tended to do.

Mavis could see the pure, unadulterated love in her eyes. She also knew that her father secretly harbored a fear that she would be an old maid; after all, she was a junior, and until this week had never had a date. She wasn't a girly-girl, and that made things take a bit longer. He'd be glad to hear it, too.

"Sit down, sit down," her mother crooned. "I'm going to make you an omelet so good, so delicious, that you won't even know there is spinach in it. Well, except for the green inside, but oh, well. I'll load it with sausage meat and cheese; it will be out of this world. You get something to drink and relax; you need your energy, girl, for that big date with that cutie. Oh, we have to get you some color; you want to be perfect!"

Mavis thought about her mother's words and went back to the mirror in the hall. As she gazed at her reflection she found she was a bit stunned; she wasn't just pale… she was white as if she had no pigment. Those red eyes made her look like one of the characters in a monster movie.

She raised her eyebrows and shrugged at her own image. Her mother would see to it she got the nutrients she needed, and maybe she would go to the tanning booth a few times. There was also a thing called 'makeup,' and that always proved to save the day, even for the most unattractive of people. Mavis decided then and there not to worry about it. She would mention tanning to her mom since homecoming was about ten days away; a week from Saturday, to be exact. She would also eat everything her mother put in front of her, no matter how yucky it was.

She returned to the kitchen and set about getting a glass of milk. "You're right, I'm downright deathly, Mom. I was thinking, maybe I could borrow a couple of your tanning sessions before the dance if you don't mind?"

Jane turned to her, spatula in hand, waving it with her words for emphasis. "Brilliant! Yes, we'll do that, too."

"Grease is flying everywhere, Mom."

The woman looked at the spatula. "Oh, yeah. Sit down, sit!"

As it turned out, breakfast was outstanding. The omelet was massive and perfect, bulging with an abundance of fillings, and Mavis had to admit that the spinach added to its flavor. She found herself wondering if she could have been wrong about the misunderstood veggie her entire life.

Cleaning her plate, including two glasses of milk and four slices of buttered jelly toast, she helped her mother by loading the dishwasher. Jane ducked out to go grocery shopping, asking if Mavis had chosen a dress with Kim for the dance. Realizing she had forgotten to give her mom the information, she fetched the sheet of paper Kim wrote up with the dress stuff and gave it to Jane so they could order it in time for homecoming.

Dishes are done, Mavis gathered her schoolbooks and cell phone and got comfortable in front of the television. She started diving into the missed homework assignments, including one for an extra book report for

Miss Hawkins, who obviously was holding a peanut butter and jelly grudge. The teacher wanted her to write a personal thesis on the lessons of *Passage of Time* to turn in before the initial book report. Boy, she had really pissed Miss Hawkins off; the teacher was famous for being easygoing and nice. For the first time, Mavis was finding out how it felt to have the tiny spinster woman's grudge, and it was terrible.

Mavis was a very intelligent girl, and she had always pulled top-of-the-line grades all her life. Catching up on two days' worth of homework was easy, and within an hour all she had left was the personal thesis, some reading of the book, and a calculus assignment remaining. She decided to take a break and make a re-heated pork chop sandwich for lunch since her mother wasn't back yet. Actually, Mavis was tempted to check out that raw liver, which had been emitting an insanely splendid aroma all the way from the kitchen. She decided against it; her mother would have her put in a straitjacket; best to just conform.

Ten minutes later, sandwich and milk in hand, she sat back down and started surfing through the television channels. A glance at the clock told her it was nearly one, so she flipped to the guide channel to see what was on; she wasn't used to watching television during weekday afternoons. Just as she settled on a rerun of a reality show, her cell started chirping.

"Hi, Kim."

"Hey," her friend said. "I'm on my way to the fifth period. Did he call?"

Mavis smiled. "Yes, and he asked me to homecoming."

"Shut up!" Her friend was screaming, and Mavis could even hear the girl's voice echo in the school hallway; she couldn't help but laugh.

"You'd probably better get to class, I guess," Mavis teased. "If you want, stop by after school. We have a lot to talk about."

"You jerk," Kim replied, and the phone went dead in Mavis' hand.

She tossed it on the footstool and said, "Yeah, I am."

∞

The rest of the afternoon went by fairly quickly. Her mother got home with tons of bags of groceries, and she made Mavis go through everything she had purchased so they could discuss iron and plan some meals together. She had brought home plenty of beef, an overabundance of liver and pork, more beans that Mavis had ever seen in one place, three boxes of bran flakes and several bags of pasta, and tons of fresh spinach, which she swore to work into every meal.

"By the time we get you well, I'm going to weigh two hundred pounds," Jane told her with a smile as they put the food away.

"I am well, Mom."

Jane flashed her a look. "I can tell by your rosy hue, Mavis."

The task didn't take long. Just as they were finishing up, the doorbell rang. Mavis shot a glance at the clock:

three fifteen.

"That'll be Kim," she mused, making her way to the door.

Jane laughed. "Wait till she gets a load of you."

Mavis turned and shot her mother a glare, laughing back sarcastically. Isn't she becoming a regular comedienne, she thought to herself, mouthing her mother's last statement for kicks. She turned the doorknob and pulled it open.

"Oh, Mavis!"

Kim dropped her books to the ground, and a couple of sheets of paper dislodged from the pages. Mavis ignored her rude best friend and began scrambling to get them. Kim just stood there, mouth agape, watching her.

When she handed them back to her, she saw that Kim was just in shock. "Well? What's the problem?"

"I... I... think I've seen a... ghost?"

"Bahahahaha!" That was Jane's laugh, loud and obnoxious, echoing in from the kitchen. "Too funny, Kim!"

"I'm glad you're adjusting, Mother!" Mavis pulled the girl into the house and closed the door. "Do you two think you could act normal for a bit? You know, just pretend to have manners and compassion?"

Jane's face immediately went serious, while Kim just continued to stare. She reached out slowly and touched Mavis' cheek, then pulled her hand away as if a snake had bitten her. After a moment, she shook her head, as if trying to snap out of a daze.

"You're… you're cold," she muttered. "Like you're dead or something."

Mavis gave a loud groan. "I'm obviously not dead, people! Now, stop!"

She looked back and forth between her mother and friend with exasperation, waiting for one of them to apologize or something. They just stared at her, and a minute passed before she gave yet another long, frustrated groan.

"Is she really cold?" Jane asked Kim as she approached her daughter. Before Mavis could do anything, her mother had taken Mavis' face into her hands and gasped loudly. "I'm taking your temperature."

Jane ran from the room, and Mavis turned to Kim and said, "Nice move, slick."

When her mother returned with the slender digital unit, Mavis told her, "Mother, I don't care what this thing says, or how I look. I'm telling you, I feel fine, okay? We just need to do what the doctors have told us, so don't freak out."

Jane ignored her and plugged her mouth with the thermometer, which gave a series of rapid beeps in less than thirty seconds. She plucked it from her daughter's mouth and read the display. "Eighty-six point five?"

"Mom, I'm fine."

"But Mavis…"

Mavis shook her head stubbornly. "Give it a couple days, okay?"

Jane stared at her for a moment, worry plastered all

over her face. At last, she said with resignation, "I'll just go make your snack." She left the room, glancing back at Mavis frequently as she went.

Kim sat down. "Wow, you look dead."

"You've made your point," Mavis replied. "Plus, you've managed to freak my mom out again, just when she was feeling better." Kim just gave her a brief shrug in reply.

"Anyway," Mavis continued, "Mom's getting my dress, and she's going to send me tanning. The iron should take care of my paleness, but we can also use a ton of makeup. I have a date with Jeff on Saturday so we can practice then. Will you help?"

"Of course." Kim put her books and purse on the sofa beside her and began to organize the escaped papers. "Seems he really likes you; I'm excited for you. It'll be weird, you know if you two become a steady item and all. I mean, we've never really had anyone… between us, you know?"

Mavis nodded.

"I can't really stay; Jacobi assigned me some extra work in calculus because my grade is slipping, and he wants it in by tomorrow." She gathered her stuff back up and stood to leave. "So, I'll call you tonight, okay? Maybe we can do something after school tomorrow."

"You can go tanning with me," Mavis suggested.

Kim agreed, and Mavis walked her to the door. When she was gone, Mavis gave a great sigh; she wished she didn't look so crappy. She wanted to go hang out with her friend, maybe even help her with her math.

The rest of the day passed quickly. Mavis spent most of her time eating, especially when she wasn't undergoing scrutiny by her parents for the way she looked. She ate everything she could get her hands on, and it seemed to appease them a bit.

Jeff and Kim both called that night, and she wound up spending more time on the phone with him than she had with her best friend. They talked about everything from music to sports to parents. Mavis thought she might be falling in love, and it was good.

She could hardly wait to see him in school on Friday and thought she'd get some makeup practice in on her own tomorrow.

CHAPTER 11

Thursday proved to be one of the craziest days of Mavis' life, in more ways than one.

First, she woke to the intense smell of food and went to the kitchen to find her mother cooking liver and eggs. While Mavis sat at the table, taking her iron supplements and drinking her milk, her mother stood over her pans, her nose crinkled in disgust. Mavis thought the food smelled outstanding, and could hardly wait for the plate, which she ended up cleaning and repeating.

Her mother gave her the card for the tanning salon and made her daughter promise to go that afternoon, with or without Kim. She agreed, actually very eager to do it. After that, Jane left to spend the day shopping with a couple of her friends but not before fawning over and nagging her daughter about how she felt.

∞

Once she was alone, Mavis finished up her calculus and got five full chapters of *Passage of Time* read, and did a bit of rough work on the accompanying report. After that, she warmed up some of the leftover liver and ate it with a spinach salad, just as her mother demanded she does.

Her pale complexion hadn't changed. As a matter of fact, it was a bit worse. She even noticed what appeared to be a bit of gray here and there, almost like streaking. She spent an hour playing with her makeup, and she knew that she would be able to pull off a normal look when the need arose.

With her confidence boosted and her peace of mind restored, she sat down to watch a little television. About ten minutes into the program she began to think about food again. Just as she stood up to find something to eat, the doorbell rang. Mavis groaned and answered the door, not caring what the person thought of how she looked. She flung it open to see a US Express delivery man holding a large, flat package.

"Can I help you?" she asked as he stared at her, dumbfounded by her looks. She repeated herself, adding, "I'm an albino; don't worry."

The man shrugged it off and made an effort to keep his eyes to himself. "I have an overnight delivery for Jane Harvey," he said as he stepped closer.

Mavis was happy to sign for it. Must be the dress, she thought as she took the electronic signature device from him. Suddenly, she smelled him. He was rich and meaty, his aroma filling her nose and clouding her brain. Her hands were trembling when she handed him back the device.

He smiled without looking at her. "Have a nice day," he said, and he turned for the street.

Mavis lost all sense of consciousness and self-control in the next few seconds. She imagined herself grabbing him from behind and sinking her teeth deep into his neck, ripping the flesh from it as she pulls away. As if she knew just what to do, putting her mouth over the wound to begin to catch the blood. Like a vampire, she would suck until he was drained and lay lifeless on the tile, spatters of blood all around him.

Without a thought, the girl knelt down. She completely lost touch with everything around her, including her present reality.

After a half-hour, she began to come to her senses. Mavis sat back and looked at what she had imagined.

She felt no remorse. It seemed that what had just occurred was normal, her nature. Mavis did feel a bit of surprise at the whole thing.

By the time her mother returned home at three, Mavis had passed the time cleaning the house for her mom. She was showered and clean, and believe it or not, her color had returned a bit. Jane was relieved and set about starting supper, whistling as she worked.

Kim showed up at four, and the girls hit the tanning salon for a session. Jane let them each use a punch on her card apiece, so they lay in their booths talking and laughing loudly about dating and boys, and they managed to make plenty of fun of old sourpuss Jacobi, the calculus teacher.

But that night, after supper and when everyone had turned in to their rooms, Mavis stood, naked, before the full-length mirror in her room. She had her door locked; after the pork chop bone incident, she didn't want to risk her mother catching her doing anything that may spark worry. All she was doing was checking out whether the tanning session had made a difference, but that was when she noticed the dark spot on her hip.

It was on the left side, a circular dark patch about an inch in diameter. Mavis touched it timidly; it felt rough, like sandpaper. With her fingernail, she began to scratch at it a little, picking at it here and there.

That was when the entire patch fell off, a chunk of gray, dead skin. It left a hole in her hip that surprised her. Mavis looked down at the chunk, which lay innocently on the floor. She knelt, picked it up, and held it to her nose. One sniff and she popped it into her mouth.

Not bad.

The hole didn't hurt at all, and to be honest, it didn't concern her in the slightest. As a matter of fact, she found it kind of amusing. Who would have thought she could be so tasty?

But her mother wouldn't be amused. She would want to drag her back to the hospital, and Mavis wasn't having it. She quickly dressed in her pajamas and vowed that she wouldn't leave the room in the morning until she had makeup on and was looking bright-eyed and bushy-tailed.

Quick calls from both Jeff and Kim put her in the mood to sleep. She dozed off quickly, thoughts of her new boyfriend in her mind. But those thoughts battled those of the piece of flesh, which had tasted like some kind of gourmet dish you see prepared on the cooking channel.

She slept the entire night through with a smile on her face.

∞

It was Friday, time to go back to school.

Mavis rose early to check her complexion. She had thought she looked better after the dream with the delivery man the day before, but as soon as she recalled the incident, she flushed. Had she really eaten that piece of flesh? She felt sort of… out of sorts about it. Not really guilty or remorseful, but more embarrassed. The way one might feel if they spilled a glass of milk in a restaurant, or tripped over their own feet in front of a lot of people. It felt sort of like… an accident.

But that was really the least of her problems that morning. One look in the mirror told her that she was right back to her pasty self. She also found another gray spot, right on her stomach next to her belly button, and the grayish streaks, which to her resembled veins somehow, seemed a bit darker as well. She checked her neck and face, but they didn't appear to be so bad that she couldn't work some cosmetic magic.

Mavis chose a long-sleeved black t-shirt which read Westside Wasps, along with a pair of jeans. The long sleeves were more of a strategic move than a choice for warmth; she didn't think she had enough foundation to cover them, and the gray streaks were a bit obvious.

At breakfast, which consisted of three heaping bowls of bran flakes for Mavis, she asked her mother for a note excusing her from gym class. Her mother didn't even question her about it; she knew it was because of the paleness that her daughter didn't want to change out, participate, and shower. If Jane was honest out loud, she didn't want anyone to see her daughter's white skin, either. She did compliment her on her makeup, however, telling Mavis that she looked like her old self.

On her way out the door, Jane asked, "Are you sure you feel up to this? Physically, I mean."

Mavis reassured her mother sincerely, hugged her, and quickly left. At the end of the sidewalk, she saw Kim approaching and breathed a sigh of relief. Just seeing her friend coming to walk with her, just like any other day, made her feel like things were truly going to get back to normal. The last few days had honestly taken more of a toll on her than she really wanted to admit.

"Hey, you!" Kim sidled up next to her and joined her at her pace. "Lookin' good, lady! Lookin' good! Things must be better with your iron level, huh?"

Mavis gave her friend an eye roll. "No, not really. Between you and me, they are actually a bit worse. What you see here is nothing more than a pound of makeup, almost literally."

"What do you mean, worse?" Kim asked, her smile gone and concern in her voice.

"Well," Mavis began slowly, weighing her words, "I actually have a couple of spots that are probably from the low iron. Nothing big, they just don't look too good. But fortunately, they are on my belly and side so my dress will hide them for the dance. Oh, yeah, my dress came yesterday. I haven't tried it on yet, but I figured I would do that tonight. Want to go look for shoes tomorrow after breakfast?"

Kim readily agreed, her attention completely diverted from Mavis' 'spots,' thanks to her love of shoes. Inwardly, Mavis breathed a sigh of relief; she probably shouldn't have mentioned the spots at all, but the way the first one sort of fell off of her in a chunk was a bit worrisome, she had to admit. Regardless of her minute anxiety over the issue, and the need to talk to a trusted soul about it, she knew that it was best to keep it under wraps. Best friend or not, she didn't believe Kim would understand. She would run to Mavis' mother, and Mavis would wind up at the Mayo Clinic as some kind of circus sideshow freak.

They walked the rest of the way to school talking about her upcoming date with Jeff the following night. They talked mostly about what she would wear, but the undertones of the conversation were giggly girl words filled with daydream ideals. Mavis wasn't going to get her hopes up; she seemed to be falling apart before her own eyes.

She had decided to wear a black, long-sleeved, open-front cropped shrug sweater with silver sequins over the dress. It would match perfectly, and cover her arms and shoulders. She would also wear silver-sheened tights, so she didn't have to worry about her legs. Mavis filled Kim in on this; the girl was disappointed because they wouldn't match perfectly, but she understood. "Anyway, it's not like I'll be your date this year, you lucky girl!" Kim replied to the revelation.

"I'm hungry," Mavis said as they climbed the stairs to the main doors of the school. "I sure hope that fixes itself soon. I had three huge bowls of cereal, and I am already thinking about lunch. Thank goodness my dad made me bring some extra snacks and gave me a note for permission. Can't wait until this is over, you know?"

No sooner were they in the door than Mavis saw Jeff. He was standing up against the wall just inside, one book in his hand, hanging casually at his side. When their eyes met, he smiled broadly, and Mavis actually saw his eyes light up. He was gorgeous!

"Hi, Jeff!" Mavis greeted in a cheerful voice.

Kim elbowed her. "Well, I'm going to run. I'll see you next period, okay? Nice to see you too, Jeff. Catch you guys later." She gave Mavis a wink and took off down the hall.

"Can I walk you to class?" he asked. "You have Hawkins first period, right? The sandwich police?"

Mavis laughed. "Good one. Yeah, Literature. I have to go to my locker first, though."

They walked to her locker and then to her second-floor class. Outside the door, Jeff stopped and turned to her, his eyes all soft and glazed like he seriously had a crush. Even Mavis saw it, and it made her entire body tingle.

"Well," he said, "here we are. Listen, how do you feel about me coming over for a while this evening, after practice, I mean. I thought maybe your parents would like a chance to get to know me better, you know? Especially your dad."

Mavis couldn't believe her ears. Jeff was quite possibly the most perfect boy in the universe. He wanted to get to know her parents, and vice-versa. He must really like her! It was music to her ears.

"That would be great! What time?" Jeff shrugged.

"Six thirty-ish?"

"Perfect."

They were so caught up in their plan-making that they didn't even notice that they were the only students left in the hall. Suddenly, Miss Hawkins opened the door to the classroom and popped her head out. Both Jeff and Mavis jumped with surprise.

"Miss Harvey!" the teacher exclaimed sarcastically. "Hope you had a good breakfast. The rest of us are patiently waiting for you; we wouldn't want to interrupt your vital conversation. You just let us know when you are ready to begin, will you?"

She shut the door a bit hard, her smile magically gone before her face disappeared entirely. Mavis smiled up at Jeff. Normally, she would have been embarrassed by the teacher's sarcastic insinuating comments, but right then she thought it was funny. Boy, for a mouse of a woman, Miss Hawkins could sure be a hag!

"Guess that's my cue," Mavis said with a chuckle.

"Yeah, I guess so." Jeff paused for a fraction of a second, then quickly leaned forward and kissed her. "Walk you to your next class?"

Her fingers went to her lips, which felt like they were on fire. With a slight smile, she replied, "Sure…"

Then he was gone.

Wow, Mavis thought. Why does he always smell like raw meat? She dipped her hand into her purse and pulled out an individually wrapped chocolate-covered cherry. Opening it, she popped it into her mouth quickly and went into class, wondering at the fact that the candy did nothing to take the scent of Jeff out of her nostrils.

It was so strong that she could almost taste him.

CHAPTER 12

The look of disappointment on Kim's face when she found out Jeff would be visiting the Harveys that evening was obvious.

"I thought I would come over and see the dress," she said in a low voice. "I wanted to see how it looked on you. I don't know if I like this 'boyfriend' crap."

Mavis felt bad; after all, Kim was her best friend and had been for the majority of their lives. "I'm sorry; I guess I didn't realize you wanted to come. If you want, I'll just cancel."

Kim shook her head. "No, don't do that. I'm just selfish. I guess it's going to take some getting used to, you know?"

"Look, your turn is next," Mavis soothed. "Who knows? Someone could ask you yet. We have a week until the dance."

Kim shrugged it off. "So, how about you show it to me tomorrow when I come over so we can go to the shoe store."

"Perfect!"

Content with their plans, they finished their walk home much more cheerfully. Mavis had noticed that day that everyone who came within smelling distance of her seemed to make her mouth water like nothing else, but she knew, deep inside, that it wasn't normal. To be honest, it felt like something of a burden, and a major distraction. But she had confidence that soon the iron would build up in her system, and all of her goofy, unheard-of symptoms would disappear; they would soon be nothing but an unbelievable memory.

Back at home, Mavis made a beeline for the fridge. Her mother was loading the dishwasher, and as soon as she saw her, she asked how the day went. Mavis scanned the shelves, the door wide open, and her appetite caused her to half-hear her mother's words.

"Oh, it was good," she replied. "What's that, in the freezer bag?"

Jane watched her closely. "Those are slices of homemade pizza that I made earlier especially for you. I won't tell you the secret ingredients, but I will say it is delicious because I had a piece. It is chock-full of iron. Heat some up, as much as you want. You'll love it."

She took out the gallon baggie and put every last piece, seven in total, on a plate and popped it into the oven, then poured a tall glass of cold milk.

"Your makeup seemed to hold up okay today," Jane observed.

Mavis slammed half the glass of milk, then topped it off again. "Speaking of which, not really. I had to touch it up constantly, and my foundation is almost gone."

"I will pick some up for you tonight on the way home," Jane replied. Your father and I are having dinner with Joe and Kathy Bakeman. What color-tone do you need?"

Mavis thought about it. "I usually use 'Creamy Natural,' but I think I'd better step it up, considering the circumstances. How about a beige? I think 'Perfect Beige' is two tones up from my normal color."

Jane jotted furiously on a small piece of paper. "Got it."

"Oh, by the way, what time are you two leaving?" Mavis asked. "Jeff is going to come over around 6:30; he wants to spend time visiting with you and dad."

"He wants to?" Jane asked with disbelief. "Where is he from, Mars?"

Mavis laughed. "I know, right?"

"Well, we aren't meeting them until eight, so that will give us an hour and a half with him," her mother replied. "I'm impressed with this young man already."

The oven bell rang, and she grabbed her plate. "I'm going to do my homework. I'll bring the plate out when I'm done. Love you, Mom."

"I love you, too, Mav. Hope this crap clears up soon."

Mavis paused and smiled reassuringly at the pretty woman with the creased brow standing before her. "I do too, Mom. I do too."

∞

Homework flew by, and before Mavis knew it, it was nearly 5:30 and her mother was calling her name.

"Yes?" she said as she walked into the kitchen, noting that her father was in his recliner, eyes fixed on the evening news.

"Todd, you need to watch that in the room," Jane yelled at her husband. "Go, get dressed! Jeff will be here in an hour, and we have to leave soon after."

Her father mumbled something unintelligible, but he didn't get up.

"Mavis, I made you a nice spinach salad with olives and mushrooms and cheese," Jane told her. "You also have your choice of a hamburger or leftover liver; pick and heat it up. Otherwise, eat what you want, okay?"

"Sure, Mom."

"Okay, I have to get ready. Why don't you try your dress on so I can see it before I go?"

Mavis thought about it; she would have to don the entire ensemble if she wanted to keep her mom from seeing her arms and legs in the state they were in.

"Um, sure."

She made her way to her room, apprehension in her heart. She was going to have to put some makeup on her chest to make sure it was covered. Ugh, she hoped her mother didn't put her under too much scrutiny and notice her little skin problem.

With her bedroom door securely locked and her overhead lights shining brightly, Mavis quickly changed. It took her about five minutes; she decided to leave her shoes off since she would be shopping for new ones the following day with Kim. Once she was finished dressing, she gave herself the once-over in the mirror: except for her pale, veiny chest, she looked good.

It took a little bit of time to cover her chest; the

makeup her mother had picked up for her was perfect. A bit too dark for the skin tone she sported before her anemia popped up, but perfect for covering up her current issues. One more glance in the mirror, and she went out to the kitchen to get Jane's approval.

She rounded the corner and went into the kitchen; her mom was standing at the dishwasher, emptying it. "Well, what do you think?" She was nervous; what if her mother picked up something she missed with the foundation?

Jane turned to her, and immediately her face and eyes lit up. "Oh, Mav! You're beautiful! Oh, that dress couldn't be more perfect, and I love the tights and shrug! Honey, I'm just so proud!"

She rushed to Mavis and threw her arms around her, embracing her. Mavis saw that her mother's eyes had teared up, and she felt nothing but happiness that, after all, her mother was finally getting to enjoy watching her daughter grow up for real. It was truly a memorable moment, no matter how simple it actually was.

"So," Mavis continued as her mother backed up and started turning her to get a better look. "This is acceptable?"

"Acceptable?" Jane repeated with a laugh. "Todd! Todd, come in the kitchen; you just have to look at this beautiful princess!"

Mavis' father appeared in boxers, a button-down, and gartered socks, and she inwardly smiled and groaned at the same time. "Wow! You're going to be the belle of the ball, little lady! Nice choice!"

He wandered off quickly, giving her an approving smile and wink. Mavis turned back to her mother. "Okay, so can I change now? Oh, and I need some money; Kim and I are going shopping for shoes tomorrow."

Jane nodded as she started rummaging through her wallet. Handing Mavis her credit card, she said, "I want you to go see Tudie at Royal Dos; I'm going to set up an appointment for you for next Saturday morning so she can fix your hair up. Oh, I can't wait to get pictures of this! I'm going to post them all over my page!"

"Mother!"

Jane flashed her a look and a smile. "It's my right as a mother, so suffer."

"Fine." Mavis went back to her room and quickly changed into her jeans and sweatshirt again. She freshened her face a bit because Jeff would be there soon. The thought made her heart skip a beat, and she wondered how long it would take to get rid of her parents so they could spend a little time alone.

Back out in the kitchen, Mavis sat and visited with her mother as she waited for Jeff. Her father, dressed and pressed, was back in front of the television watching a hunting show and every now and then he would burst out laughing at some unknown joke.

Mavis was a bit nervous that Jeff would either change his mind and call or simply not show up at all. After all, this was a pretty big undertaking for a teenaged young man who had taken her on one date. It was actually a very mature suggestion, and it made

Mavis want to believe he was honestly and truly interested in having a relationship of some kind with her.

But she had nothing to worry about: at six twenty-four on the dot, the doorbell rang. She jumped up and began talking rapidly. "Oh, my, he's here. I'll get it." She ran through the living room, cutting off her father, who had already gotten up to answer it. She turned to him. "Sit! And don't embarrass me, and don't talk about the iron problem, okay?"

Her parents looked at her as if she had lost her mind. The bell rang again, but she just stood there for a moment, holding the knob and breathing in and out. Finally, she opened the door to the freshly showered young football player.

"Hi, Mavis!"

She smiled shyly. "Hi. Come on in."

He stepped through the door, and she turned to make the introductions, but he beat her to it. "Nice to see you again, Mr. and Mrs. Harvey. Hope you don't mind me stopping by to visit."

Jane put her arm around the boy and led him to Todd's recliner because it was the best seat in the house. Todd's mouth dropped open in surprise, but he plopped down at the end of the sofa and kept quiet. "Have a seat, dear. What can I get you to drink? Soda? Iced tea? Water?"

Jeff smiled politely. "Water's fine. I stay away from caffeine during football season."

"Smart boy," Jane replied. "Water it is." She left the

room to get his drink.

Mavis sat in her mother's rocker. "My Mom and Dad are going to dinner with friends in an hour. They were happy to spend some time visiting with you though."

She could tell Jeff was a bit nervous, but he handled it well. Something inside of her told her to give him and her father a minute alone. "I'm going to go help mom. Dad, what do you want to drink?" She flashed him a look that said 'just pick something!' He wasn't much of a beverage sipper.

"Um… I guess… water?"

She left them alone in the room and went to the kitchen. "Dad wants water, too," she told Jane. "Let's just all have something, okay? I think he's a little nervous."

Jane plucked three more glasses out of the cupboard and filled them with ice from the refrigerator dispenser. "Of course, he's nervous," she replied. "This is a huge thing for a young man his age, and at his own suggestion! But, Mavis, he is such a cutie!"

The girl groaned and smiled dreamily. "I know. Isn't he, though?"

Her mother handed her two of the filled and chilled glasses. "We'll duck out a bit early to give you two some time alone. I know that I can trust you to be responsible, yes?"

"Of course, Mom," she replied with an eye roll. Secretly, though, she was thrilled that they might leave a bit earlier.

They walked into the living room to find both Todd and Jeff laughing and discussing bow hunting like old pals. Jane sat next to her husband on the sofa, allowing her daughter to sit closer to Jeff in the rocker. They remained quiet and let the guys bond over the TV show for about ten minutes, then, true to form, Jane took the reins.

"Okay, boys," she stated as she nodded toward the remote. "Time to shut it down."

Mavis caught the cue and turned off the television since the remote was on her dad's end table between her and Jeff. Jane continued, "So, Jeff, tell us about school and football."

For the next ten minutes, they talked about his grades, his favorite subject, and his love of sports. Next came a discussion of his family; he lived with his mom, dad, and three sisters, all of whom attended college at the University of Ohio. This led to questions about his future plans.

Jeff wanted to study medicine, but he wasn't going to go to his family's alma mater if he could help it. He had his heart set on attending the University of Iowa first because he felt it would best prepare him for Stanford, where he would decide on his specialty. At the current time, however, he wanted to be a pediatrician. Mavis sat and listened to him, her face proud and glowing, and she knew she was completely smitten.

Her parents were so impressed with him and enjoyed their conversation so much that they nearly lost track of time. It was nearly seven-thirty before her mother realized it, and when the woman finally jumped up and pulled Todd to his feet, Mavis was relieved. Finally, they were going away!

Jeff stood as well, and Todd held out his hand to the young man. "Mr. Deason, I have to say, I am very impressed with you and the goals you have for yourself. I have absolutely no problem with you and my daughter being… friends, or dating, or whatever."

Everyone laughed nervously, and then Jane gave the boy a big hug. "We're going, now. You two behave; Mavis, in bed before midnight, if we're not home, okay?"

The girl nodded, and just like that, her parents were gone.

Once the car was out of the driveway, Mavis watched through the curtains, she turned to Jeff. "So, we have some time… alone, I guess. Do you want to watch a movie?"

Together they decided on a romantic comedy called *Crazy Love*; she hadn't seen it, but he had, and he said for a chick flick it was good. They sat next to each other on the sofa, holding hands, watching and laughing.

Jeff was very respectful; he didn't try to make a move or take advantage at all. But Mavis, on the other hand, was in bad shape. She could smell him, and she found that she was really worked up. She didn't know for sure, but she thought she was turned on. It didn't take long, and she was the one making the moves.

She laid her head on his shoulder first; Jeff put his arm around her in response, and they continued to watch the movie. But in seconds, his scent overwhelmed her, and her head began to cloud up. She began to softly kiss his neck, and she could hear his breathing pick up quickly. After several of her kisses to the neck, Jeff gave a soft moan and began to squirm a bit.

He looked at her, the movie was all but forgotten. They stared into each other's eyes for a long moment, then, slowly, he leaned forward, and his lips met hers. The two began to kiss in earnest.

Mavis was really getting excited. In fact, she was pressing herself against him and running her fingers through his hair. He began to stroke her back as their kisses got more heated, and before she knew it, she was straddling his lap. She had never felt like that in her life.

But the funny thing, and it was something she was all too aware of, was the fact that 'Jeff' was not what was on her mind. As she inhaled his scent and tasted his mouth, she wasn't thinking about him being a boy. She wasn't even thinking about sex. The thing that she was thinking, the thing that had her so worked up and was on her mind was… Meat. Jeff was meat. That was all she could think.

But she wasn't properly aware of this thinking. It seemed normal, and she was going to go with it. She buried her face in his neck and began to nibble and lick here and there, and she could feel his excitement, but it meant nothing. Then, she opened her mouth, and she was getting ready to give him a good nibble in earnest; she had lost her judgment.

That was when his cell phone began to ring.

Jeff jumped, and Mavis groaned loudly, getting off his lap so he could fish the phone out of his pocket.

"Hello?" He spoke for a couple of minutes, and she knew it was one of his parents.

When he hung up, he looked at her and smiled with regret. "I have to go, beautiful. I have to take my aunt to the pharmacy before it closes. See you tomorrow?"

Mavis was bummed, but she kept it to herself. "Ya, see you."

At the door, he turned to her. He gave her a quick kiss and said, "I think I love you."

Then he left her standing there, staring at his car as it drove away.

CHAPTER 13

Mavis woke early on Saturday, refreshed and very excited about her date with Jeff that evening.

She dressed and spent time on her makeup since she would go shopping with Kim a bit later. She thought that since her parents were out so late, having not returned by the time she went to bed, that they would sleep in. But to her surprise, she found Jane in the kitchen reading the paper in her bathrobe.

"Morning," Mavis greeted as she opened the fridge. "Dad still sleeping?"

Jane looked up as she sipped her coffee and gave her daughter smiling eyes. "No, he went with some guy from work. They're golfing. Your breakfast is in the pan on the stove. You look good, well-rested. How did it go last night?"

Mavis went all dreamy again. "Amazing." She piled the food on her plate and put it on the table, turning to pour milk. "We watched a movie, but he didn't get to finish it; he had to leave to run an errand for his aunt. But, I must say, it was awesome." She sat down and took her iron pill, then said shyly, "So, what do you think?"

"We love him, Mav," Jane replied, pushing the paper aside. "What a kid, huh?"

Mavis sat back and smiled, her fork in hand. "I know, right?"

"So, what are your plans today?"

Picking up her fork, the girl replied, "Kim and I are going for shoes, and we'll likely have lunch out if that's okay. Jeff and I are going out tonight when he's done with practice."

"What are you doing?" Jane asked.

Mavis was chewing, so she picked up the pace, answering just after she had re-loaded her fork with the potato and egg mixture her mother had whipped up. "I think to eat and just hang out. He mentioned some specifics, but I was in shock so bad I really don't remember." She shoveled her massive bite into her mouth.

"Did you two kids kiss?"

Mavis spit her food all over the place, choking. After taking a long drink of milk, she said, "Mom!"

"Well!"

Mavis shrugged and reloaded her plate as Jane grabbed a paper towel and cleaned up the mess. "I guess... yeah, okay. It was awesome."

"No sex, though, right?"

Her daughter rolled her eyes and shook her head. "No, Mom. Kind of hard to afford med school if you are taking care of a child or paying child support. We're both smarter than that, and we've had only one date, for crying out loud."

Jane gave a chuckle, then stood drinking the last of her coffee. "I'm going to shower and dress. I'm volunteering at the women's shelter today; they're doing the free clothes giveaway. So, I likely won't be back until this afternoon. I won't worry about your lunch; use the card to pay for you and Kim both, but she can buy her own shoes, Mavis."

"Okay, Mom," she replied with her mouth full.

Alone, she finished her breakfast and then, still hungry, stood at the counter eating three pieces of cold leftover pizza. It all filled her stomach more than sufficiently, but her mind was focused entirely on the smells that she had been overwhelmed with lately. Mavis realized, standing right there eating cold spinach pizza, that the word 'meat,' which she had been using to describe the odor, was entirely wrong.

The smell was simple: Fresh.

The revelation made her heart pound somewhat. It wasn't normal to think about human flesh as delicious food, and her mind told her that. But something else inside of her pushed that truth aside. Regardless of her natural logic, something told her it was perfectly normal for what she had become.

But whatever that was, she didn't know.

The telephone rang, which prompted her to look at the clock: nine-thirty. She snatched it out of its charger and pressed the button. It was Kim, calling to warn her that she was on the way over.

"Hello?"

"Hey, Mav," her friend greeted her. "What's

happening? I'm walking to your place right now."

Mavis swallowed the last bite of pizza. "I'm ready. Just finished breakfast. Oh, and Mom said I could buy lunch, so the sky's the limit."

"Sounds good," Kim replied cheerfully. "See you in a bit."

They disconnected, and Mavis went to her room to grab her purse, which was already stocked with Mom's platinum card. She ran a brush through her hair, checked her makeup, and tucked her foundation into her purse in case of an emergency. On her way out of her room she grabbed her jacket, then closed the door firmly behind her. Jane was leaving her own room at the same time.

"Getting ready to leave?" her mother asked.

Mavis nodded. "Kim will be here any second. Do you want me to bring anything back from the store for you?"

Jane shook her head. "I feel bad that you two are on foot today," she said. "I would've let you take the car, but I have volunteering today. I'll tell you what: why don't you give me a call when you're done? I'll duck out long enough to give you two a ride home."

She shook her head. "Thanks anyway. The walk will be good for us, and it's a nice day. Besides, with me being suspended last week, and then with the time I've spent with Jeff, I think that Kim has been feeling a bit left out. Walking will give us more quality time than if we had wheels, you know?"

As if on cue, the doorbell rang, and after greetings

between her mother and friend, the two girls were off for their day on the town.

"Where do you want to go first?" Mavis asked.

Kim's eyes lit up. "I thought that new shoe place, 'Heelz,' down at the strip mall on Davis Avenue, would be a great place to start. Bethany said they have the best formal shoes and purses ever!"

"Oh, man! I've wanted to check that place out," Mavis agreed. "Heelz it is!"

They walked in silence for a couple of minutes, then Kim asked, "So, did you talk to Jeff yesterday?"

Immediately, Mavis felt the blood rush to her cheeks. "Yes," she replied.

"Well?"

"He came over last night, you know, to get to know Mom and Dad," she continued. "They loved him, and then they actually left, and we had a bit of time together... alone."

Kim stopped in her tracks and turned abruptly to Mavis, her eyes alight with excitement. "What did you guys do? Did you get some?"

"Get some? Wow, Kim." Mavis shook her head and laughed. "If you mean kisses, and a little hot and bothered, then yes. But other than that, no! You can be so vulgar!"

They started walking again; they were going to catch the bus two blocks away, which would take them right by the strip mall on Davis Avenue. "Come on, Mav. If you got all 'hot and bothered,' then you know exactly what I'm talking about."

"Okay, fine," she agreed. "But we are having our second date tonight; it's a bit early to be going the distance. After all, he's the first boy I've ever dated at all. Neither one of us are sluts, you know."

"What are you two doing tonight?" Kim asked.

With a shrug, Mavis said, "I guess just going out to eat, then just hanging out."

They reached the deserted bus stop and plopped down on the bench; they had a few minutes until it arrived.

"You know," Kim said slowly, "I have to tell you something."

Mavis glanced at her, then checked to make sure her cell phone was in her purse. "What's up?"

"Well, I guess I'm feeling a little guilty. You know, about you and Jeff."

That caught Mavis' attention. "What do you mean, guilty? Why?"

Kim shrugged, embarrassed. "I guess I'm jealous."

"You like Jeff?" Mavis asked, her tone filled with surprise. "Kim, why haven't you said anything?"

Her friend shook her head. "No. I don't like Jeff, not like that. I'm… I'm jealous of you. The time we used to spend. I know it isn't major, but if you guys get serious…" Her voice trailed off.

Mavis got it right away. Her best friend, the girl she had spent years confiding in and hanging with and gossiping too, was feeling left out. She was lonely, and she was getting a picture of what adulthood was going to mean for their friendship. Right then, for the first time, Mavis got it, too.

"I can see your point," she replied in a low voice. "I'll do my best not to make you feel forgotten, Kim."

She wrapped her arm around the girl and gave her a partial embrace. Kim smiled and leaned her head on her shoulder in response. When she looked back up at her, there were a couple of tears in her eyes, but Mavis could tell that she felt reassured.

"Sorry I'm an idiot," she muttered, brushing at her eyes.

Mavis shook her head. "No, Kim. If the tables were turned, I would be scared too."

The bus pulled up, and laughing with relief, the girls climbed aboard, putting the seriousness of the moment far behind them.

∞

That Saturday turned out to be one of the most personal and memorable days of their friendship.

Both of them found the shoes they wanted; matching, of course, at 'Heelz.' They were simple, black satin pumps with silver sequins sewn over the toes in a feminine, flowery pattern that was perfect for the dresses they had chosen. They also chose tiny silver clasp purses that were on sale for the grand opening of the store. Mavis paid for Kim's, making a mental note to tell her mother and promise to pay it back.

They visited a couple of other shops in the mall just to pass the time and have fun: one was a novelty store with cheap little gag gifts, magic tricks, and the like. Another was a tropical pet shop, which sold everything from birds to snakes. By the time they left the pet shop, it was lunch time, and Mavis was nothing less than ravenous.

They settled on fast food for lunch. Donnie's burger joint just across the street from the strip mall, and they happened to have a triple-bacon cheeseburger they called 'Mount Bacon', and it was Mavis' favorite. Kim, who loved food more than life, watched her friend wolf it down and go order another, her eyes wide with disbelief. After all, she didn't make it half-way through hers, and she was full.

"Have you gained any weight?" she asked. "You know since you started eating more?"

Mavis shook her head and swallowed her last bite. She wiped her mouth and sat back, rubbing her stomach. "I mean, I haven't weighed myself, but my clothes haven't gotten any tighter. As a matter of fact," she plucked at the jeans she was wearing, "they almost seem… looser. I was thinking about that this morning. I don't get it; oh, well."

"Well," Kim stated with her nose in the air after taking a noisy slurp of her pop, "I think you're a jerk. Say it like you see it, my dad always says."

Both of them burst out laughing, causing other diners to turn and look in their direction. They quieted themselves, threw away their trash, and left the restaurant giggling, bags in hand.

They caught the bus going home, talking about homecoming all the way. During the ride, Mavis' cell rang. She looked at the screen and saw that it was Jeff.

"Hey! What's up?" she greeted him.

"Hi, beautiful," he responded. "I don't have much time to talk; I just got to practice. Listen, I have a friend on the team, a close friend, actually. Shawn Maher, do you know him?"

Mavis thought she did. "Yes, I think so."

"Well," Jeff continued. "He doesn't have a date for homecoming. He knows who Kim is, and he wondered if she'd be interested. If she is, will you give me her number so he can ask her? You can text it to me."

Mavis was excited. This was perfect! Shawn Maher was a good-looking guy with dark hair and pretty brown eyes. He was a halfback on the team and considered fairly popular. She had never seen him with a girl, but she never thought about it, either.

"Absolutely! That's awesome! I'm with her now, so I'll let you know soon." She paused and blushed. "I had a good time last night."

Jeff chuckled. "Me, too. By the way, our plans have changed. If it's okay with you, my parents would like it if you came over for dinner tonight."

She immediately got nervous.

"Hey, are you there?"

Mavis snapped out of it. "Yeah. Yes. That would be fine. What time will you pick me up?"

"Six thirty, right after practice. Is that okay?"

"Sure," she replied. "Perfect. Have a good practice."

"See you then, cutie." He said hanging up.

Mavis stared down at her phone. "What's up?" Kim asked.

"Oh, nothing," she said as she stuffed her phone into her purse. "We're eating with Jeff's parents tonight; change of plans. Oh, and something for you."

"What?"

Mavis turned to her friend, a smile covering her face. "Shawn Maher, from the football team? He wonders if you want to go to homecoming with him, and if so, can I give Jeff your number for him?"

Kim stared at her, eyes wide. "Shut up. You're lying."

Mavis shook her head. "No, I'm not! I would never lie to you about something like that!" She paused, and a grin broke out on her face. "We'll get to double-date... together!"

Both girls let out excited screams, startling all the other passengers on the bus.

"If you girls don't keep it down, you can get off right here and walk home!" the driver yelled. "You're going to make me crash! I mean it, now!"

"Sorry," they both said in unison, then they broke out in giggles.

When it died down, Kim whispered, "Yes! Text Jeff my number now!"

Mavis dug out her phone and hurried to carry out the task. Who would have ever guessed that in their junior year they would both get their first dates, and they would get to attend homecoming, with boys, together! She was thrilled.

It was all so perfect.

Once the girls got off the bus, Kim walked Mavis home from the stop, but she didn't want to stay. She was so excited about the date with Shawn Maher, and she couldn't wait to tell her mother. He ended up calling her during a break at practice, just when they arrived at Mavis' door, and asking her officially. The girl was almost in tears, and she wanted to go home.

∞

So, Mavis found herself alone in the house. Both of her parents were still gone, and she was hungry once again. She had a craving, but not for food; she wanted flesh, but what could she do? It seemed she had no control over herself, and it seemed… okay.

But what would people think? What about her mother and father? She would go to prison if anyone ever found out; she had the brains and sense to know that murder was wrong. Then why did it seem so… right?

So, for the first time since she got 'sick,' Mavis found herself having something of a moral dilemma about her condition. For someone who was so ill, why did she feel so fabulous, so strong and energetic? Granted, her physical appearance, without makeup, was lacking, but she felt spectacular, and she couldn't seem to reconcile the two in her mind.

She pushed it all out of her mind; she'd be fine. That was when she got a brilliant idea: she would hop on down to Flair Foods and get herself some raw meat of her own. She'd stick to beef, to not make herself worse, maybe beef liver, and she'd keep it in the little cooler in the basement. She'd load the thing with ice and put it in her room for her little meaty snacks. Perfect!

Mavis rode her bike to the grocery, which was about four blocks away. She chose a couple of steaks and some raw liver, all beautiful cuts, nice and bloody. She paid with her own cash stash rather than use her mother's card; that would result in a bust for sure.

Back at home, Mavis got out the little cooler that her dad used to use to take lunch to work. She filled it with ice from the kitchen dispenser and buried her meat in the bottom. The girl was flooded with relief. Not only would she have deliciousness whenever she wanted, but it would also keep her from having a breakdown, or whatever incident that could happen.

By four her mother still wasn't home, so she showered and began to get ready for her date with Jeff: dinner with his parents. It wouldn't be so bad; at least his sisters were away at school. Mavis didn't feel ready to meet siblings, not quite yet.

She chose a pair of her favorite jeans, which were nearly new, and a loose, gypsy-type top, with lots of lace and long poet's sleeves. It would provide excellent coverage, and she would look casual and comfortable, yet pretty at the same time. It would be ideal for the occasion. She didn't want to appear too stuffy; she wanted to be herself as best as she could.

By six, she was completely ready, and she stood looking at herself in the mirror. For the first time, she felt completely soft, feminine, and attractive. She loved her appearance, and she thought that Jeff would, too.

Her mother walked in just as she was putting her cell in her purse. "Mavis, you look great! What are you two doing? Do you know for sure?"

Mavis nodded as she sat at the table to visit with her mother and wait for her date. "Yes. Plans changed. We're eating with his parents tonight."

Jane turned to her and gave her a scolding look. "Listen here, young lady. That boy came here to visit us of his own accord. You'd better change your attitude. One hand washes the other, you know. That's what relationships are all about, missy!"

"I know, Mom I'm just worried."

The doorbell rang, and Mavis nearly fell out of her chair. She was far more nervous than she thought, and while her mother answered it, she breathed in and out and looked at herself in the mirror obsessively. She couldn't look better, and it was time to pull herself together.

Jeff and Jane stood at the door chatting when she appeared. "I'm ready if you are."

Jeff smiled at her. "You look awesome." He offered his elbow, and she took it. "We're off, Mrs. Harvey. I'll have her home on time."

Jane nodded. "Have fun, kids. Mav, you'll be fine."

They walked out to the car together in the twilight, both nervous, but both very happy.

CHAPTER 14

Max and Meg Deason were the most down-to-Earth, easy-going parents (next to her own), that Mavis had ever met.

They welcomed her into their home with warm hugs, crooning over her appearance. They insisted she call them by their first names, and they sat her down with a cold soda in the best chair in the living room, just as her parents had done for Jeff. It took seconds for her to feel relaxed, almost as if she were right where she belonged.

They wanted to hear all about her. School, personal interests, plans for the future, all of it. They told her about themselves and cracked jokes that were actually funny. In no time, Mavis felt just like one of the family.

They had a simple meal of fried chicken, loaded mashed potatoes, and salad. For dessert was chocolate caramel cake, and it was sinful. Mavis ate until she was packed full and could hardly move. Her hunger, for the first time in ten days, was completely gone. All that was left behind was a nagging, confusing urge in her brain that seemed to constantly pull her mind toward flesh. She ignored it the best she could.

Around ten, Jeff announced they were going to take a drive before he delivered Mavis to her parents. Hugs were exchanged, and extensive insistence that she comes more often. It turned out that she really liked the Deasons; now if only things worked out with Jeff.

"So," he said once he had the car on the road, "what do you want to do? We have an hour."

Mavis gave him a shy grin. "Maybe we could park at Zander Point, you know, just to look at the lights."

His return smile was enough confirmation for her. They stopped briefly at the Halt and Hop convenience store for drinks, then made their way to the traditional parking area, located on the highest hill of the city. The view from there was spectacular, not that any of the parkers were usually paying attention.

The place was packed, and Jeff wound up taking a crappy space where tree limbs got in the way of the view, but neither of them mentioned it. Mavis had other things on her mind anyway; she was looking forward to his kisses and his smell. As soon as he put the car in park and turned in his seat, Mavis threw herself in his arms, her lips right on his.

It started off slow, but soon the two teens were panting and groping a little too much. Even though Mavis could feel his excitement, her mind was far from the actual making out. He was gently caressing her breast, but she was about to be overcome with the urge to sink her teeth into his neck.

Her lips left his, and she trailed slow, soft kisses across his cheek. She pecked at his earlobe, then sucked it gently. That was about all it took.

Quickly, she moved her mouth to his neck and bared her teeth slightly, her mind gone and a slight smile of anticipation on her face. Jeff was breathing loudly now, and even moaning a bit. His head was back, and his eyes were closed in the throes of pleasure.

Knock, knock!

Mavis froze, her smile fading; did someone just knock on the window?

The raps came again, this time more insistent.

"Mavis, someone's knocking. Stop, babe."

She pulled away and sat back hard in her seat, exasperated enough to kill. But her mind was clearing as Jeff rolled down the window, and suddenly she realized what she had been getting ready to do. Once again, confusion came over her, but this time it was accompanied by a tinge of fear.

"Hey, dude! What's up?"

It was some guy at the window. She recognized him from school, and she knew he was on the football team. He was a friend of Jeff's, obviously, but who interrupted someone who was making out at a make-out spot?

Jeff sighed and adjusted himself in his seat. "Hey, Brian. Just brought my girl. Have you met Mavis?"

The two acknowledged each other, then Brian the genius turned his attention back to Jeff. "Didn't mean to bother you, man. Rhonda and I saw your car, and we'd never seen you up here on the Point before. I just had to come to see if it was really you. So, how you feel about the big game next Saturday? We haven't really talked about it, but I'm feeling super-pumped, dude. Let's kill Westchester!"

Jeff gave a half-hearted chuckle, and Mavis could tell he was as frustrated as she was. Only she knew it was for a different reason, and the personal knowledge made her self-conscious. Shouldn't she be sexually frustrated? Not frustrated like someone had interrupted a starving person's meal? Weird.

"Yeah, man. We'll kill 'em." Jeff flicked on the dome light and looked at his watch. "Hey, sorry I can't talk longer, but we gotta get going. I'll see you on Monday, okay?"

"Yeah, okay dude," Brian said, his oafish smile glued on his face like a mask. He gave Mavis half a wave. "Nice to meet you."

"You, too."

When he was gone, Jeff let out a loud sigh. "Sorry. It's late; better get going, huh? We can't catch a break."

Mavis smiled and fastened her seat belt. They left the Point with the music playing, holding hands. Something inside her told her that Jeff was concerned that she was upset. She had taken his hand to reassure him, and he had eagerly accepted it with a smile.

In her driveway, he turned to her and gave her a lingering, but safe, kiss. "Can I call you tomorrow?"

She grinned. "You'd better."

Mavis got out of the car feeling surprising relief. She had been getting ready to do something that she never wanted to do. Good thing that moron Brian had knocked. She wasn't mad at all, just a little confused.

Did she almost bite Jeff's neck?

Mavis knew it, and it freaked her out a little.

∞

"So, kiddo, tell me all about it."

As soon as Mavis walked in, her mother hit her up. She was in her blue silk pajamas reading a magazine in the lamplight in her rocker. Mavis was willing to bet she had been there waiting for hours, or at least since her dad went to bed.

She gave her mom a big smile. "How about I go change into my 'jammies, and then I will."

Jane jumped up. "Want some cocoa? Or warm milk? I'll get it ready if you do."

"Cocoa would be awesome, Mom."

She went to her room and picked her gray Westside sweatpants and t-shirt, along with her slippers. Mavis changed quickly, her emotions torn. She felt out of this world about Jeff; he was like a dream come true. But what the heck was really going on with her? It was getting harder and harder to believe she just had low iron problems.

She shuffled into the living room, changed and cozy. In a couple of minutes, Jane came out of the kitchen with two steaming cups topped with an abundance of marshmallows.

"I know it's not winter, but this stuff always warms my belly and helps me sleep." She handed her daughter one cup, then made herself comfortable in the rocker. "You know that, don't you? I think I've told you that a hundred times in your life."

"A thousand." They had a good laugh, then sipped their cocoa for a bit.

After a couple of drinks, Mavis set her cup down; her mother had already put hers on the table, and now she was sitting cross-legged in her rocker, leaning forward like an eager teenager. Mavis looked at her, amused.

"So?" Jane pressed.

Mavis sat back in her father's recliner, her eyes all misty and goofy. "It was amazing; they were amazing. I can't believe this is finally happening to me!"

She spent the next hour telling her mother all about Max and Meg Deason. They talked about what they ate and talked about, and Mavis couldn't brag them up enough. She knew that her parents would like them; they might even be good friends.

Next, Mavis filled her in on going to Zander Point and told her about kissing a little. She also relayed the bit about Brian's little interruption, and the two of them had a good laugh about that as well. She even went so far as to tell her mom about Jeff saying he thought he loved her.

But deep in her heart, none of that really mattered; she wished she could tell her mom about the weird place her head was at.

She skipped it, though, and the two of them had the best night together, just a girl's night of talking, laughing and too much cocoa. Mavis had a warmed-over plate of leftovers from her parents' supper, and at around one in the morning, they finally hit the sack.

She put all of her concerns out of her mind as she lay in her bed, and that night Mavis slept like a baby.

R.W.K. Clark

CHAPTER 15

Sundays around the Harvey house were extremely routine.

The mornings were always slow, consisting of hours in pajamas in front of the television, eating food off of TV trays, and hair that hadn't been brushed. In the afternoon, they would head on over to her Grandma Cabot's house, and they would have supper, and Mavis would watch her grandmother have too much wine and listen to her dirty jokes; it was a riot. Sunday actually had always been one of Mavis' favorite days of the week all of her life; she loved her parents and grandmother, and Sunday mornings and afternoons were like a traditional bonding time that all of them looked forward to.

But this Sunday proved to be different, for the first time in her life. She couldn't sit still in the morning, and her mother kept giving her odd looks because she was fully dressed and made up. At her grandmother's house, that evening all she could think about was going home and diving into her meat cooler. She was distant, and when her family tried to talk to her about the anemia, or Jeff, or the upcoming dance. She often missed their words, not hearing or answering.

In the car on the way home, Jane asked her, gently and with concern, "Are you feeling all right, Mav? I'm kind of worried; you just don't seem to be yourself."

Magically, Mavis didn't have to think about a response. It was as if her brain was ready with an answer, and she even surprised herself. She gave her mother a smile and said, "I'm fine. Don't worry, Mom."

Her mother had been satisfied.

Once they were home, Mavis told her mother she was going right to bed; she wanted to be full of pep for school the next day. She got no arguments, and went right to her room and locked herself in. She spent the next two hours tearing through the meat in her cooler, wiping it out completely. Mavis made a mental note to take a backpack to school the next day and stop at the store for more of it on the way home.

By the time she washed her hands and brushed her teeth in the bathroom, her parents were in bed; she could hear her father's content snoring, and it made her smile. They were sleeping; now she could relax and sleep herself, knowing that they hadn't heard her slurping and sucking on that food in her room. She shook her head at the fact that she even had to worry about it.

Mavis looked forward to the following day; it was one step closer to the big dance, the highlight of her life.

∞

Jeff called her bright and early, way before she had even left for school. Mavis was still eating her eggs and bacon when her mother handed her the phone with a grin. She had to rush to swallow the large lump of food in her mouth.

"Good morning, Jeff," she said lightly.

"Good morning to you," he replied cheerfully. "I tried to call you yesterday; did you get my message?"

Mavis paused; she hardly even looked at her cell on Sundays, but Jeff wouldn't know about that. "Oh, I haven't. Sundays are a big family day for us; we go to my grandmother's, and I usually leave my phone at home."

"Oh," he said. "Sorry; I didn't know."

"It's not a big deal."

He cleared his throat. "I just wanted to apologize for that stupid Brian again; he's a jock with a jock's brain if you know what I mean."

"Don't sweat it, Jeff," she said. "I put it out of my mind. Will I see you at school today?"

He paused. "Well, that was another reason I'm calling. I have to go to Cleveland with my family today. My uncle is having major surgery, so we are all going to be at the hospital to support him. I probably won't be back until Wednesday, and then I have to put in extra practice time to make up for the absence before the big game. It's going to be a busy week, and I won't get to see you much, but I'll call every chance I get."

"I hope so," she said. "Will he be all right?"

"Yeah, we think so." He didn't sound too sure. "He has kidney problems, and this isn't his first surgery, but we're hopeful."

"I'll keep you in my thoughts."

Jeff paused again; this pause seemed heavy. "Okay. I love you."

His bold statement stunned her.

"Mavis?"

She jerked out of it. "Yes, you too. See you when you get back, and talk to you soon."

She hung up and started eating again, ignoring the fact that her mother was staring at her.

"Did he say, 'I love you'? Just like that?"

Mavis looked up at her, chewing, and nodded.

"You didn't say it back, I noticed," Jane muttered lightly as she began to wipe the already-clean countertop.

Mavis swallowed her food. "Just a little too soon, I think."

The subject was dropped. Jane made sure that Mavis took her iron, and she handed her a baggie full of cold pizza rolls to snack on during school. When Mavis packed her duffel bag, she stuffed them in as well and made sure to take some extra cash for her meat.

School seemed to be a real drag that day. She finished *Passage of Time* while in Lit class and even managed to wrap up the personal thesis Miss Hawkins had dished down as punishment for the incident with Tommy Johnson's lunch. She got three-quarters of the way through the book report, and she thought it was one of the best things she had ever written. Her brain felt sharp and fast, even though her heart was heavy. It felt good, however, to know she would turn in the assignment, along with the extra one, to her teacher before anyone else. That should get her back into Miss Hawkins' good graces.

Before science, she stopped in the restroom and checked her makeup. She wanted a bit more black eyeliner, so she added it. She had never really worn a lot of eyeliner, but as she observed the dark lines around her eyes, she found it appealed greatly to her. It actually set off the makeup, making the subtle, covered-up pastiness look… attractive.

After second period science, she and Kim headed for the restroom again, this time so her friend could go herself. They used the restroom on the second floor at the end of the hall; it wasn't one that they normally visited. As they approached the door, both of them heard a ruckus going on inside.

Mavis shot Kim a look, and they entered.

There, in the very back of the room by the last stall, were two girls. One of them was Shanice Hall; she was stuck-up and had a reputation for being something of a bully to those she considered 'less' than herself. She had the other girl's back against the wall.

The other one was Donna Reilly. Donna came from a poor family and often had to wear the same clothing two or three days in a row. She didn't have nice shoes or even the money for makeup, and she got a lot of flack for those facts. But she was sweet and kind, and she wouldn't hurt a fly, even if it hurt her first.

Shanice was in Donna's face. She didn't hear Kim and Mavis come in; she was too busy calling Donna

'Dumpy Donna' and poking her in the chest with her forefinger. Tears were running down Donna's cheeks, and she refused to reply. The poor girl was trembling with fear and embarrassment.

Shanice ripped the girl's purse from her hands and began to rummage through it. She pulled out a pad and waved it in Donna's face. "Are you a bleeder? How about I punch you and see how you really bleed?"

Mavis had had enough.

"Hey!"

Shanice spun around, smiling when she saw the girls. "Aw, screw you too. When I'm done with her, I'll get to you."

Kim glanced up at Mavis. Normally, they would have left it at that. But she saw something she had never seen before: Mavis was smiling, her eyes all lit up.

Mavis just continued to smile. She looked casually around the bathroom as if admiring the décor and then began to stroll toward Shanice and Donna. She trailed her fingers over each of the sinks as she passed them as if she was feeling some fine material or something.

"How have you been, Donna?" Mavis asked casually, ignoring Shanice.

Donna looked stunned. "F-F-Fine."

Shanice laughed at the girl and poked her chest again. "F-F-Fine," she mocked.

Mavis laughed, too. The bell went off in the hall, and Kim looked panicked. She wasn't about to leave her friend, though, so she pushed it out of her mind; detention it would be.

Mavis' laughter tapered off. She stopped about two feet from the confrontation and crossed over to the stalls; there, she leaned back against one of the narrow panels separating the stalls and crossed her arms over her shoulders. Setting her eyes dead on Shanice, she held her smile.

"It's fun to pick on Donna Reilly, you think?" she asked.

Shanice studied her, then nodded. "You know it."

Another laugh, this one a bit deeper, and tinged with anger. Kim saw Donna's eyes widen. Mavis wrapped up her laugh with a sigh.

Suddenly, Mavis shot forward and gave Shanice a shove. She pushed her so hard that Shanice's feet left the ground; she flew into the last sink, hit it, and dropped to the floor like a sack of lead, a big 'oof!' shooting from her mouth.

Mavis walked calmly to her and knelt down. She leaned forward, putting her face inches from the bully's; Shanice had had the wind knocked out of her, and she was trying to catch her breath.

"You see," Mavis began in a low, somewhat evil voice, "I think it's fun to put cruel little girls like you in their place. I think it's very satisfying to show you how you make other people feel." She extended her forefinger and poked Shanice in the chest with each of her next words. "What–do–you–think–of–it–now?"

The bully's eyes were fixed on her, and they were beginning to water.

"Do you want to punch me, Shanice? Do you want

to back me up against the wall and call me names?"
Mavis laughed. "Come on, now, don't quit so soon. The
party is just getting started."

Donna Reilly gathered her scattered books and ran
from the restroom like a scared rabbit.

"Well?"

Shanice just stared.

Mavis stood and gave the girl a boot to the thigh.
"Get up."

Shanice struggled to her feet, a sob escaping her lips.

"Now," Mavis continued. "You might think you are
going to get Donna back on account of this little
incident. You might even be planning on trying to
corner me. Well, I will come to your house while you're
sleeping, and I'll rip your jugular out with my teeth.
Then I'll pack you in a garbage bag, and I'll take you
home and save you for a late-night bite, you little self-
righteous bully. If I were you, I'd reconsider."

Shanice didn't even give it a second thought. She
grabbed her purse and books out of the basin of the
sink, where she had placed them. After giving Mavis a
look of terror, she fled from the restroom as fast as she
could go.

Mavis didn't say a word to her stunned best friend.
She simply went into one of the stalls and started to pee.
Kim had completely forgotten that she needed to go;
she even had to look down to make sure she hadn't wet
herself.

When Mavis came out and began to wash her hands,
Kim said, "Mavis? What the heck?"

Mavis shrugged and plucked a brown paper towel from the dispenser. "I'm sick of girls like that, aren't you? Didn't you see Donna's eyes? She was petrified. Well, Shanice Hall won't be bothering her again."

She grabbed up her own books and looked at Kim expectantly. "Well? Did you pee? You said you had to pee."

Mavis' words didn't even register; she just nodded at her friend.

"Well, come on, then," she continued. "We're gonna have to get passes to get into the class because we missed the bell."

∞

As it turned out, tough-girl Shanice Hall had left the restroom and run directly to the principal's office whining and crying that she had been beaten up by Mavis Harvey.

When Mavis and Kim arrived at the office to request passes, they were both hauled into Principal Pearson's office. There sat the bully of the year, crying and playing the ultimate victim. Kim was horrified; Mavis was amused.

"So, Miss Harvey, our 'late bloomer' when it comes to trouble." Mr. Pearson's voice was stern. "Would you care to explain what took place in the second-floor girls' room?"

Mavis gave Kim a glance. "Sure. But first, let me clarify that Kim was completely an innocent bystander. You should let her go."

"I'll decide that when we are through here."

Mavis shrugged and looked over at Shanice, giving her a smile and a wink. "Kim and I went into the restroom to... well, use it. This monster over here had Donna Reilly backed up against the wall; she was calling her names, poking her hard in the chest with her finger, and just being cruel. I mean, Mr. Pearson, the poor girl was crying!"

The principal shot a look at Shanice, who was suddenly interested in something going on outside.

"Go on," he told Mavis.

"Well, sir, it made me sick," she continued. "Yes, I pushed her away from Donna, and yes, I said some things that would prompt her to consider what it would be like if the tables were turned. I'm willing to take a punishment. But this girl is a vile human being; I hope you bring Donna in here and ask her about it, as well. She is the real victim here, sir."

Kim sat in stunned silence, nothing to say at all. Mavis said her piece and sat back, and Shanice was suddenly preoccupied with picking invisible lint off of her blue jeans. Mr. Pearson gave them looks all around.

He pressed the button on the intercom on his desk. "Mrs. Fordyce, would you please call Donna Reilly to see me?"

"Yes, sir."

He turned to Shanice, whose tears had magically dried up. "Is this true, Miss Hall?"

She shot him a glare and kept her mouth shut.

Mr. Pearson sat back and steepled his fingers under his chin. "If Miss Reilly confirms these accusations, Miss Hall, you have some nerve coming here crying to me. I will be motivated to hit you with as much suspension time that is within my power." He turned to Mavis. "As for you, if you are telling the truth, I must commend you for your bravery, but you will still be punished for taking matters into your own hands. I'm surprised at you, Mavis. Getting in trouble, twice in two weeks! Do I have to meet with your parents?"

She shrugged. "Any consequence you give me, sir, will be a pleasure." She shot another look at Shanice, who was now staring at the ceiling.

They sat in silence for two or three minutes, until a knock came at the door. Donna Reilly entered the office, shaking like a leaf and white as a ghost. The first person she saw was Shanice, and she froze. Then she saw Mavis, and she visibly relaxed, even smiling slightly.

"Have a seat, Miss Reilly." She sat.

Mr. Pearson leaned forward. "Tell me about what happened in the restroom."

∞

Twenty minutes later Mavis was walking home to do another two-days suspension. Kim had been returned to class with Donna, and Shanice was walking home on the opposite side of the street to do two full weeks herself. Mavis kept a close eye on the bully, trying to make her as uncomfortable as possible until she turned down Macon Street and disappeared out of sight.

Mavis began to hum; it had been a very productive day.

CHAPTER 16

She stood outside the front door to her house, took a deep breath, turned the knob, and walked in.

There stood Jane in the kitchen doorway, leaning against the jamb. Her arms were crossed, and her face was serious. Mavis just closed the door and stood there.

"I don't know whether to punish you or hug you," her mother said.

Mavis simply replied, "A hug would be nice."

Jane just threw her hands up and walked over to embrace her daughter. Mavis let her. She felt overwhelmed and wanted to cry. She felt exhausted and confused by her own behavior. Since when had she been the one to fight for the underdog? She was usually the underdog herself!

Jane stepped back and looked at her. "Let's get you something to eat, and you can tell me all about it. I'll decide then."

She fed Mavis spaghetti and meatballs from a can, along with sliced bread toasted and smeared with garlic butter. Mavis ate a pile of it while telling her mother the entire story of Donna Reilly and Shanice Hall, and she left nothing out. She even told her she kicked the girl in the leg when she was down.

She thought her mother would be furious, but the woman was beaming with pride by the time she was through.

"Definitely worth a two-day suspension, and I think that's punishment enough, don't you?" she asked.

The girl nodded, relieved.

"Now," Jane continued, "I have to go. Melody Pratt and I are delivering meals to the elderly. Will you be okay alone? I'll be back by two."

"I'll be fine, Mom."

Not long after her mother left, Mavis' cell buzzed; it was a text from Jeff asking if she could talk. She spent the next half-hour relaying the school confrontation to him and listening to his cheers of support. When it was time to hang up, he told her what an awesome girlfriend she was, and once again told her he loved her; this time she reciprocated.

When the call was over, Mavis was overcome with exhaustion. She lay down in her room, thinking about the nerve she had suddenly gotten in the girls' restroom. It scared her somewhat, and something inside of her told her that it had to do with the anemia. Something much more profound was going on with Mavis, and she knew it.

∞

"So, do you think Shanice will try to sic her friends on us?"

Kim and Mavis were in Mavis' room sitting cross-legged on the floor playing a board game. Kim had come over right after she took her books home and filled her mother in on what had happened. She had come back because she wanted to find out if Mavis was okay; after all, she just wasn't herself lately.

"I don't care if she does," Mavis replied with a sneer. "As a matter of fact, I hope she tries it. I would get more joy from getting in their collective faces than ever before in my life."

Kim looked at her in disbelief. "But a whole group of them?"

Mavis thought about it. "You know what? I'm not afraid; that's the funny part."

"I'd say," Kim replied. "Mavis, what's going on with you lately?"

The girl flopped back onto the floor, the game was forgotten. "I don't know, Kim. I just don't know, but something is. Is it really all bad, though? I mean, it's not like I'm hurting people." She kept the thoughts of the delivery man to herself.

"I guess you're right," her friend said. "It just seems like such a drastic change in such a short amount of time. I mean, you're like completely opposite of normal, you know?"

"I know." She sat back up and studied her friend. "Guess you're back to walking to school alone for a couple of days. Sorry."

Kim gave her a smirk. "It was worth it. Seeing that mean girl cry was like a birthday gift."

They both burst out laughing. The fact was that almost every girl in school had been victimized at one time or another by Shanice Hall, and it had been going on since kindergarten. Mavis didn't know how the girl would act in the future; what she did know was that if she ever saw her doing that to someone again, she would turn her into a casserole. It might have been a joke to Kim and Donna, but Mavis meant it with her entire heart.

They put away the game and found a good movie to watch. Kim stayed for supper for the first time in a while, and it felt good to have her best friend around. Mavis was feeling a bit unsteady and unsure lately; having her there made everything seem normal, just like it had been a mere two weeks ago.

She left early, with homework to finish and school the next day. Mavis turned in early, too. She had completely forgotten, with all the drama, to go to the grocery store for meat, so she dug in the fridge and took a full pack of bologna to her room to munch on. She finished up her homework and fell asleep by nine.

That night, Mavis dreamed of Shanice Hall on a platter with a big red apple in her mouth.

CHAPTER 17

Mavis woke up Tuesday morning feeling like a new person. She thought briefly of the incident in the school restroom. The memory made her smile, and she felt absolutely no shame. As a matter of fact, she was a bit proud of herself. She made a mental note to see how Donna was doing when she returned to school on Thursday.

For breakfast, Jane had outdone herself: she made a 'shipwreck' consisting of scrambled eggs, hash browns, peppers, onions, cheese, and mushrooms all fried together in a pan. She had prepared a huge mass of it, and to her surprise, Mavis ate more than half.

"What are your plans, Mav?" Jane was loading the dishwasher, and Mavis was scrolling through her Social Media accounts. "You're not grounded, so you are free to do what you want today. I'm going to spend the day with Grandma if you want to come."

Mavis was initially tempted; it would be good to hang out with the girls. But then she remembered her much-needed trip for meat, and she opted out. "Kim brought me my assignments for the next two days when she came last night; I'm going to work on that, I think."

Her mother was pleased with her responsible decision and didn't press the issue. Once the kitchen was cleaned up, Jane left, and Mavis made a beeline for the market. With her purse slung over her shoulder, she walked with her face in the sun, feeling like a million bucks.

She strolled the four blocks to the store with not a care in the world. When she arrived, she chose the finest, tastiest, and bloodiest meat she could find and quickly made the purchase. Mavis left the store whistling and thinking about the rest of her day: she would go home, lock herself in her room, snack on some liver, and hit that homework. Just because she had hit a couple of bumps in the road didn't mean she would be letting her grades suffer; she had plans for the future, after all.

Two blocks from the store, Mavis got the feeling that someone was following her.

She stopped and spun around; the street was milling with people, and none of them seemed to take any notice of her. Mavis focused and scanned the area twice, but saw nothing. Finally, she shrugged and continued on her way.

Mavis didn't get another half-block. Just as she was preparing to pass the Smiths' large privacy fence and cross the alley behind her house, someone grabbed her from behind and pulled her into the alley violently. She stumbled under the force and hit the ground hard, rocks and other gravel bits tearing at her shirt and skinning her face.

She was lying on her back trying to get her wits about her. When she opened her eyes the first thing she saw was the silhouettes of two people, the sun shining brightly behind them. She couldn't make out their faces.

"What the…"

"I'll bet that's what you're thinking!" a girl's voice said.

The person grabbed her arm and jerked her to her feet. Stunned, her hand went to the scrape on her face as she focused her eyes on the faces of those before her. It took her a minute to see her assailants.

They were Shanice Hall and her best friend, Candy Wilkes.

Mavis didn't skip a beat; she smiled and said to Candy, "What did you do? Skip school to be a gorilla for your slave driver?"

That was when everything went haywire. Candy reached out and shoved Mavis into the Smiths' fence, thinking it would put her down again. Mavis knew they were planning to tag team her and beat the crap out of her, but she wasn't afraid.

As soon as her back hit the fence, she let the bag of meat fall to the concrete, and she lunged forward with a roar. She hit Shanice full-force, knocking her to the ground and slamming her head on the pavement. Mavis straddled her and looked her in the eyes, smiling broadly.

The girl smelled better than the liver.

Like lightning, she leaned forward and sank her teeth into the bully's cheek. The blood that rushed into her mouth tasted so good that she didn't feel any of the kicks that Candy Wilkes was delivering to her legs. But then the girl hit her with a kick to the ribs, and that pissed Mavis off. How dare this girl interrupting her when she was eating?

She turned to Candy, blood all over her lips and chin, and smiled at her as well.

Candy let out a scream so shrill that a passerby would have thought she was being attacked herself. She took off running, and that was when the first pedestrians started to wander in the direction of the chaos they were hearing. Mavis snapped out of it right away and realized that Shanice was screaming like a banshee, her hand on her cheek, blood seeping through her fingers.

She rolled off the girl and flopped to the ground. "Help! Help me!" she screamed. "They've attacked me! Help!"

People were running toward them now, and Shanice was scrambling madly to her feet. She took off in the other direction, down the length of the alley. An old lady arrived and knelt down by Mavis; she saw the blood and panicked.

"Call 911!" she yelled.

"No! I'm not bleeding," Mavis told her. "Those girls were kicking and punching me, and I bit that one; it's her blood!"

Now the old lady pointed in the direction that Shanice had run. "Stop that girl! She attacked this child!"

Mavis sat up, shaking a bit, but lucid and in her right mind. She was pissed, though, and she was going to see to it that those girls paid for this. She dragged her shirtsleeve across her mouth and saw the blood, then her eyes went to the bag of meat, resting on the ground feet from where she sat.

She stood and grabbed it up, stuffing it into her purse. "Are the police coming?" She asked.

A man with red hair and glasses who was standing nearby said, "I just called them; they're on their way."

Mavis lifted her shirt and saw a large purple bruise forming over her ribs and side. It was blocking out the pasty skin and veins; her mother would want to take her to the hospital. She knew she would refuse, but she was going to press charges on those evil witches for sure. Her right thigh throbbed as well from the kicks Candy had delivered. She would let the police photograph the injuries and blame the gray streaks and stuff on the wounds. They were in so much trouble, and it pleased Mavis to no end.

She thought about Shanice's cheek but chose not to worry. It was a bite, and she had to defend herself. With the reputation those two had, it would go as smooth as silk. They had it coming; they had to be the vilest human beings Mavis had ever encountered if indeed they were human beings at all.

The police showed up in what seemed like only seconds. She was interviewed in the back of the car and then taken to the station for a statement and photos. They urged her to go for medical attention, but she refused, so they just called her mother to come down and assist in the charging process. All in all, it took about two hours to deal with the red tape, and before she and her mother left the station, the police sent a squad to pick up the violent delinquents.

On the ride home, her mother fawned and fussed. Mavis didn't complain; she was exhausted, and she was worried about the warm meat in her purse. She would eat it anyway, as soon as she got home. It certainly wasn't going to go to waste. Something inside of her knew that she would feel better as soon as she got it inside of her belly; it was the cure.

"Mavis, I just don't know what to think." Jane was practically in tears as she drove. "Everything seems to be lining up so wonderfully for you, but it all seems to be falling apart at the same time; I just don't get it!"

"They attacked me, Mom," Mavis replied in a dull, lifeless voice.

Jane shook her head and went silent. After a minute, she said, "I know that; that wasn't what I meant. It's just that all of this is happening at once: the anemia, the peanut butter sandwich situation, the pork chop bone, Jeff, and now these horrible girls… it's just so much to take!"

Mavis tensed up, but she kept her wits about her.

"Fine," Mavis replied as she put her head back against the headrest. "I just want to go home and soak in a long, hot bath, okay? Whatever comes, well, I'll deal with it as it comes."

Jane looked at her daughter lovingly and reached

over to pat her on the thigh. "You are such a good, responsible girl. Look at you! Sticking up for that poor Donna, and this is what you get. I certainly hope the police pick that juvenile delinquent up as soon as possible before she hurts anyone else."

Mavis watched the houses pass through her window. "Don't worry. You should see her. Believe me, I left her with quite a reminder."

Her mother chuckled. "That's how it sounds, and I'm not a bit upset about it. A little brat is what that girl is."

"She's more than a brat, Mom; she's a freaking criminal."

∞

Mavis and her mother weren't home more than twenty minutes when the police called; Shanice Hall and Candy Wilkes had both been arrested.

While it was a relief for Mavis because they deserved it, it almost felt a little bittersweet; she would have liked to have them for dinner, so to speak. After all, they certainly deserved that, too. No matter how black her soul was, Shanice's blood was sweet.

The thought made Mavis smile.

She filled the tub with steaming hot water; she needed a good soak. Her mother opted to stay home with her instead of returning to Grandma Cabot's. Jane wanted to be there for Mavis in case there were any after-effects of the attack; she was concerned about internal bleeding. Mavis knew her mother's worry was all for nothing. She was a bit bruised, but she was fine otherwise.

The bath felt amazing; she soaked in it for a good hour. Once the water started to cool off too much, she got out, dried off, and put on her robe. Her mother was making lunch for her, and she was ravenous. She was thankful that she thought to put her meat away as soon as she got home, and reminded herself to put fresh ice in the cooler as soon as she had a bit of time alone. It really didn't matter, though; Mavis knew she would eat it no matter what.

While she was putting her makeup on, her phone started ringing. She glanced over at the device sitting on her vanity: it was Kim. A glance at the clock told her it was lunch period, so she wasn't surprised; probably calling just to see how she was, or to gossip.

She hadn't even gotten 'hello' out of her mouth when her friend started talking, and a hundred miles per hour, at that.

"Oh, my, Mavis. Jenny Wong said that Curtis Maines told her that his best friend Roger texted him and told him that while his mother was driving him back to school from a doctor appointment that he saw you in an alley, surrounded by cops, with blood all over your face. What in the heck?"

Mavis couldn't help it; she cracked up laughing immediately. She laughed so loud and long that her mother put her head in the door, concern on her face until she saw the phone in her hand. The woman rolled her eyes and closed the door.

"It's not funny, Mav," Kim said, perturbed. "So,

what's up? Are you okay?"

"Yeah, yeah. Don't worry." She walked over to her bed and lay down, her bruised rib causing her to move a little slowly. "I was walking home from the market when that stupid little tramp Shanice and her friend Candy pulled me in the alley and tried to beat me up, that's all."

"Oh, my!"

Mavis chuckled again, this time wincing from the bruise. "Don't worry; I got the best of them. Candy managed to plant a few good kicks on me, but I messed up Shanice's face really bad; I nearly bit her cheek right off. It was great."

"Are you in trouble?" Kim asked.

"Ha!" Mavis replied. "Not me. The cops called it self-defense. A bunch of people started running toward us, and they took off. Someone called the police, and when they saw the bruises I had they took me to the station, called my mom, and we filed charges. They just called about an hour ago and said both of those idiots were arrested. Serves them right."

"Jeez, Mavis, that's insane!" The girl sounded blown away. "Listen, you want to do homework together tonight?"

Mavis didn't have to think about it; she could use the company. "Sure; I still have some assignments left to make up. I have to finish my Lit report and a couple of other things, so that sounds good." She paused. "Listen: don't tell anyone at school, okay? Let them ramble. I don't want Jeff to get any false information from his friends. I'll tell him when he calls me."

"Isn't he out of town?"

"Yeah, but he talks to his teammates," she replied. "He'll be back Wednesday for school, and he'll be busy making up practice time, but I'm sure word will get to him anyway. I expect him to call; I'll fill him in then."

Kim agreed. "I gotta go. See you later."

"Later."

Mavis went back to her vanity, definitely moving a bit slower than usual. She finished her makeup. When she was done, she observed her reflection. She really liked the excessive eyeliner. Maybe the pale look wasn't so bad, but until she got her mother used to it, she would use foundation. She simply would use less and less to break Jane in.

∞

"I felt like treating you," her mother told her over her shoulder when Mavis entered the kitchen. "Big lunch: steak, baked potato, baked beans. Sound good?"

"Amazing."

Mavis poured a glass of milk and sat down. "Mom, I don't want you to worry. It's only a couple of bruises, and it was well worth it if it got those two in trouble, believe me. I've never met such a black-hearted person in my life. Seriously."

Jane put her daughter's plate down in front of her and sat down with her own. "Well, Mavis, that's all fine and dandy, but you're my daughter, and I love you. The thought of someone hurting you infuriates me. You'll understand when you have a child of your own."

Mavis looked at her. "I love you, Mom."

Jane smiled. "I love you, too sweetie."

For the next half-hour, the two of them ate together, enjoying each other's company, and talking about anything and everything except the alley incident. Jane wanted to return to Grandma Cabot's, but this time she insisted that Mavis go with her. Mavis was tempted to argue, but she knew that, with what had happened, it was best to just comply, for her mother's sake. She understood that Jane didn't want to leave her alone.

With lunch over and the dishwasher loaded, the two of them left the house, eager to put the day's events behind them, but first, they would have to deal with filling in Grandma Cabot.

CHAPTER 18

Mavis' Grandma Cabot was her mother's mom, and she was one of the most fun and unique people Mavis knew.

She loved bright colored clothing and floppy hats with big fake flowers on them. She wore too much eyeshadow and bright red or pink lipstick, depending on her mood, and her blush was always in eye-popping circles on her cheeks. She was funny and energetic, and Mavis thought she was beautiful.

When they first arrived at her house, her grandmother hurried them inside and poured them iced teas, doting over Mavis because of the health 'problems' she'd been having. According to her, Mavis looked beautiful, not sick at all. Mavis thought she might get away with not talking about the morning's incident, but she soon knew better.

They took their drinks out to the patio and sat down at the table with the umbrella. "So," Grandma Cabot said after sipping her tea. "What was this situation with the police that your mother had to rush off for, Mavis?"

Mavis threw a quick glare at her mother, who pretended not to notice. "It was nothing, Grandma. I'm not in any trouble, and I'm fine."

"Well, if it's nothing then you won't mind filling me in, little missy."

Mavis sighed and sat back; might as well start at the beginning, because she wasn't going to get out of it. "Monday at school I walked in the bathroom, and a girl was bullying another girl. Well, I sort of took matters into my own hands, and I got a suspension."

Her grandma removed her glasses and started to polish the lenses with the hem of her shirt. "Now, I'm aware of that; your mother tells me everything. After all, I'm her mother, and we are best friends. She was here this morning, after all. What does that have to do with the police?"

"I went up to the market to get a soda and some chocolate." She felt okay about leaving the detail about the meat out. "When I was on my way home, the bully from the bathroom and her friend were hiding in the alley, and they sort of jumped me."

"Oh, my! Are you okay?"

Mavis smiled a little. "Of course, I'm okay, Grandma. You see me, don't you?"

Jane interrupted. "She has a huge bruise on her side, and some others on her legs; the police had to take pictures, Mom!"

"Oh, Mavis! Let me see!"

Mavis groaned. "Grandma, no! It looks worse than it is, and you'll just get yourself all worked up. Listen, I got the best of that little… well, you know. Also, the police called us when we got home, and told us both of them had been arrested. Just relax."

Grandma Cabot gave Jane a look, and Jane shrugged in return. "She says she's fine, Mom. It's not like she's two; we have to trust that she can tell if she is hurting abnormally, or whatever."

"Well, that's just dandy." Grandma Cabot turned to Mavis. "If you turn out to really be hurt, I will never let you live it down, missy. Do you understand? I just don't get you kids today, thinking you are all grown, fighting in alleyways, and picking on other kids. Well, at least you interfered. I can rest in peace at the fact that you have some morals, anyway."

They lapsed into silence, and the subject was dropped.

For the rest of the afternoon, the three of them worked in her grandmother's garden, picking ripe vegetables and weeding. Soon, it would be time to pull all the plants to prepare for the fall tilling, and Mavis and her mother would return for that as well.

When they were finished, her grandmother gave her some fresh chocolate chip cookies with milk and packed a large baggie full of the sweet treats for her to take home. Afterward, she scolded Mavis for not seeing the doctor one more time, then kissed the girl all over her face, leaving bright pink lip prints everywhere; she did the same to Jane, and the two wound up sitting in the driveway wiping it off with tissues for ten minutes before they drove away.

Regardless of her grandma's eccentricities, Mavis and her mother both drove away smiling.

"Mr. Pearson pulled me into the office after school today."

Kim and Mavis had just finished up with their homework, and they were lounging around her room waiting for supper to be called. Kim would be eating at home, but she didn't want to leave until she had to. For now, they would take the time to hang out together.

"Why didn't you tell me that before?" Mavis asked, annoyed.

Kim shrugged. "I don't know. Anyway, he heard about the thing with Shanice in the ally through the grapevine as well, and he wanted to know if I knew anything. You know, since we're besties and all."

Mavis groaned. "I guess; what did you tell him?"

"The truth, as you told it to me." Kim turned to the vanity mirror and started to pick at her face. "He was furious; he said he has had it with 'that girl.' I don't think he meant you."

"He didn't."

Mavis' cell rang; it was Jeff.

She told Kim who it was, smiling, then answered the line. She tried to keep her voice light and cheerful. It wouldn't do to make him think she was on her deathbed breathing her last breath. She didn't want that kind of attention from him because she was a big girl who could handle her own business.

"Why didn't you call me earlier?" he asked right away.

Mavis crinkled her nose. "Why?"

Jeff growled. "Brian texted me that you got jumped by Shanice."

Now she rolled her eyes. "I'm fine, Jeff; no worries. Besides, she got busted for it anyway. Don't let it freak you out. I've got a couple of bruises, but I'm fine."

"Well, I wish you would feel comfortable enough to talk to me about stuff," he continued. "Anyway, we'll be leaving tomorrow morning instead of tomorrow night, so I'll be home around lunch. Can I come over? You'll be home, right?"

She agreed and went through the 'I love you' thing before telling him she couldn't wait to see him and would talk to him the following day.

"Mavis, when I listen to you talk to him you don't really sound very enthused," Kim observed when they had hung up. "Don't you like him?"

"Sure!" she sat up on her bed. "I enjoy his company, he's gorgeous, and I love having a boyfriend. It's just that…"

"What?"

Mavis shrugged. "He's already talking about love; I just guess I'll feel more comfortable with it once more time has passed."

The truth was that she couldn't seem to reconcile her emotions to her physical temptation to taste his flesh. That just didn't spell love, in her opinion. She chalked it up to the anemia, and just need more time.

Jane called dinner then, and Kim took off to her own house. Mavis ate quickly, excusing herself once her father had been filled in on all the drama that had taken place that day. She told them she still had make-up homework to do, but that had been a lie. The truth was, she wanted to put her pajamas on, watch a movie on her laptop, and wait for her parents to go to bed so she could clean and empty the old water out of the cooler and put fresh ice in it for her meat.

The rest of the evening passed quickly, and her parents turned in fairly early. Mavis was able to take care of the ice problem in no time once they were shut up in their room. When that was behind her, she was overcome with exhaustion. She nestled herself under the blankets, closing her eyes.

She fell asleep thinking about Jeff, and the odd cravings for the food she had developed that seemed to be rapidly growing out of her control.

CHAPTER 19

Much to her surprise, Mavis and her mother received a late-morning visit from the principal of Westside High, Mr. Pearson.

She should have expected it, but since the incident with Shanice Hall and her friend hadn't taken place on school grounds, it was the furthest thing from her mind. He showed up after they had their breakfast, while they were filling the dishwasher. Jane answered the door and let him in right away, offering coffee, which she already had made.

Mr. Pearson sat at the kitchen table with them both, steaming coffee cup in hand.

"Who can we thank for this visit, Hal?" Jane began once they were all comfortable. He had gone to high school with both of her parents, so he and Jane were on a first-name basis.

Mr. Pearson cleared his throat. "Well, I wanted to get Mavis' side of the incident yesterday. I know it has nothing to do with school, but if Mavis is going to have some kind of restraining order against Miss Hall, I would be more than happy to expel the girl, eager even. She is a bad seed, Jane."

Mavis hadn't wanted a restraining order, though the police had recommended it, and her mother had pushed her. She wasn't about to cower from such a person and actually looked forward to seeing the girl in school again. But now that Mr. Pearson mentioned expulsion, she began to think about all the other kids whose lives would be made easier by the bully's absence.

"We didn't get a restraining order, sir," Mavis began. "I'm not afraid of her; that's the main reason. But if expelling her means that all the other kids she harasses would be safe, I am willing to do it. They said I had seventy-two hours to pursue one if I changed my mind."

A look of relief came over Jane's face. "I wish you would, Mavis, afraid or not. If that girl had the audacity to pull you into an alley for a beating, and her friend was willing to skip school to help, who knows what other lengths they are willing to go to? What if they actually break into our home, or vandalize it? Kids today can do much worse, as you well know."

Mr. Pearson wanted the details of the attack. After agreeing to go to the courthouse with her mom to file for the order, she told him all that had happened, down to the last detail. Why shouldn't she admit to biting her? She didn't have to tell them she was going to eat her just that she was trying to protect herself from the evil girl.

He listened intently, shaking his head frequently with disgust. When she had finished, Mr. Pearson took a deep breath and sat back in his chair, thoughtful as he fiddled with his empty coffee cup. Jane rose to fill it, but he stopped her, saying he had enough.

"I think it is more than reasonable to expel Miss Hall, restraining order or not. You are the victim here, and to have her return to class with you there as well would be callous, not to mention unprofessional." He rose and stretched slightly. "My mind is made up. For your sake, and her sake as well, get that order, Mavis. This girl needs to have consequences if she is ever to mature properly and become a productive adult in this society."

He gave her a pat on the back, as she stood up, Mavis and her mother then walked him to the door.

"I'll see you tomorrow," he said. "I'd have you return today, but I really want you to go to the courthouse and take care of this issue."

With a pat on Mavis' back and a shake of her mother's hand, Mr. Pearson was gone.

Jane turned to her. "Get your purse. We're going now."

Mavis rolled her eyes and obeyed.

The entire process at the courthouse took just over an hour. This was mostly due to the fact that Jane had remembered to bring their copy of the police report and copies of the photos of her injuries that the cops had provided them with for that very purpose. They filled out the papers and saw a judge, who took one look at the paperwork and granted the order. He also made them aware that both girls had been released from detention to the custody of their parents, with court dates pending. If either of them came within three hundred feet of Mavis, they would be arrested again, once the violation was reported, of course.

From there, they took copies of the order to Mr. Pearson at the high school, who appeared to be happier than he should be about kicking the bullies out of Westside permanently. That didn't matter, though; Mavis knew many kids who would be far happier than he. Happier and safer.

When they got to the house, Jeff was waiting in the driveway.

"I tried to call you, but you didn't answer," he greeted.

Mavis smiled and gave him a peck on the cheek. "I left my phone at home; we were at the courthouse getting a restraining order against Shanice."

Jane put her key in the door. "We're getting ready to have a late lunch, Jeff. Have you eaten?"

He smiled. "Yeah, but I can always eat, Mrs. Harvey. I'll have to leave after that, though. I have to go to school and finish today's classes, then I'm tied up with practice until eight tonight. Gotta be ready for homecoming."

For lunch, her mother made sandwiches with carrots, celery, and potato chips. Mavis tried her hardest to control herself, but she wound up eating two sandwiches anyway. Jeff seemed to be more amused by her appetite than anything.

The three of them talked about the incident in the alleyway, as well as Mr. Pearson's visit. Jeff was glad about the restraining order, but not for the same reasons as Mavis. He wanted her safe, just as her mother did. Mavis already knew she was safe; it was other people she was worried about. Shanice didn't scare her; she knew if she had ten minutes alone with the girl she would turn her into a full meal.

Mavis walked Jeff to the car, leaning to give him a kiss. She kept it brief, not wanting to stir up her appetite again. Her little meat stash was helping her to ease her mind; Jane thought the starving behavior was ebbing a bit, and Mavis didn't want to wind her up again. She quickly kissed him and told him to call her that night when he got home if he wanted to; otherwise, she would see him in school the following day.

Mavis spent the rest of the afternoon helping her mother with housework. They dusted, vacuumed, did the laundry and ironing, and even washed the kitchen windows, which seemed to get dirty faster than any others in the house. By the time her father got home dinner was nearly made, and the table was set and ready.

But dinner didn't satisfy Mavis, not even slightly. She soaked in the tub again, turned in early, and locked herself in her bedroom. Mavis spent the next three hours, until well after eleven, watching movies on her computer and eating raw liver. The entire incident with Shanice and Candy was out of her mind; she no longer cared at all. It was time for her to move on, just as it was time for everyone else to do the same.

Besides, she thought as she wiped bright red blood from her mouth, she had other, much more important things to worry about.

CHAPTER 20

When Mavis returned to school the following day, she was in for a big surprise.

It all began when she and Kim started climbing the steps to the building: everyone in the yard and on the steps, even those crossing the street, began to cheer. She could hear her name being yelled, along with plenty of 'Go get 'em' and 'Yeah, girl' statements being hollered. She received unexpected pats on the back, and it seemed that she couldn't even walk through the halls without being stopped and complimented, even thanked.

It seemed Mavis was now Westside High's new hero.

Everyone was her friend, even people she didn't know. They showered her with attention, and they crowded her to the point of claustrophobia between each and every class. It was very uncomfortable and overwhelming, and by the time she was finished with the fifth period, Mavis couldn't take anymore.

She made her way to the office, asking to see Mr. Pearson as soon as possible.

Once she filled him in on what was going on, the

man didn't hesitate. He had his secretary run to her final two classes and get the day's assignments, and he sent her home. He also promised he would make an end-of-the-day announcement over the intercom to the entire school, explaining that he understood their appreciation for her standing up for what was right, but that she really needed to be able to get from class to class without being bothered too much. Mavis was relieved, and she ducked out of the building as quickly as possible.

With a little free time on her hands, she was able to stop at the market and reload on her liver, which had become her all-time favorite meat. It blew her away that less than a month ago she wouldn't have touched the stuff, and now she wanted it raw and bloody. Her mother would be appalled!

Mavis took a long way home. She wanted time alone to process and think. She wanted to think about Jeff and the dance; she wanted to think about her new food choices and how strange they were. But most of all she just wanted to be alone, without anyone trying to talk to her, kiss her, or fret over her well-being.

Mavis was tired of it.

So, she walked. She walked until after four, which was a full hour after she usually returned home. She wasn't concerned about whether or not her mother was worrying; Mavis would just tell her she wanted to be alone and take a walk.

But, to her surprise, her mother was not worried. She thought that Mavis being late was exactly what it was, especially since Mr. Pearson had called her as soon as Mavis left the building. That was why she hadn't bothered to call her cell or bother her.

"How about we play some cards or something, Mavis," Jane suggested. "Let's just have some nice, relaxing time together. We won't talk about any problems; we'll just sit and have fun."

The suggestion sounded awesome to Mavis. She turned the ringer off on her cell and put the device in her room. Jane brought out crackers, cheese, and summer sausage, and together they sat, played rummy, and ate their hearts out. They did think of Todd, however; he would be hungry when he got home, so half-way through their card game they took out a frozen pizza, doctored it up with goodies, and popped it into the oven.

After all of them had eaten, they watched television together. The reality show *Superstar*, which was more or less a talent show with the promise of fame for the winner, was a big hit. Usually, Mavis didn't indulge in watching, but that evening it was amazing. They laughed, gave their opinions, and thoroughly enjoyed each other's company.

It felt like old times if one could consider thirty days ago 'old times.'

Mavis did. It seemed as if the month that had passed since her anemia set in was equal to a lifetime. It seemed that in the last weeks she had matured, to an extent. She was quieter, less 'girly' in her behavior, and much more introspective. Maybe it was because of the raw meat obsession, but she wasn't the same person, and she knew it. True, she couldn't put her finger on why, but she knew it anyway.

Right before the news started at ten, Mavis thanked her parents for a great evening. She gave them both kisses and hugs, then went to her room. It was time for her private snack, and she wanted to go over the two minor assignments the teachers had sent her home with. She knew she could complete them before bed, no problem.

Regardless of all the weirdness and changes, Mavis found that she was very content. Sure, she felt like she had to keep most everything about her 'new self' a secret because other people wouldn't understand. She felt normal, strong, and healthy. She didn't want things to change.

She had just finished up her homework when Jeff called. It was after eleven by then, and he was worried that he was waking her, but she reassured him he wasn't. Actually, Mavis was glad to hear from him; she saw that she had missed his call while watching TV.

"I'm looking forward to Saturday," he said. "Are you coming to the game?"

"Of course," she replied. "I wouldn't miss it."

He paused. "Sorry, you had to leave school early. If it's any consolation, every last student is glad Shanice is gone."

"I'm not sorry." She wasn't. "It was worth it. People like her shouldn't be allowed to mingle with others. I mean, criminals get separated from society, and that's what she is: a criminal."

Jeff laughed. "Isn't that the truth? Well, at any rate, I want you to know that I'm proud of you. I'm proud of you for standing up to her, and I'm proud of you for fighting back when she attacked you. Most of all, I'm proud of you for getting that order, even though I know you didn't want to."

"How do you know that?"

"Because you aren't the kind of girl to hide," he said. "I love you; goodnight, Mavis."

With that, he quickly hung up. She hadn't even had a chance to respond, and it surprised her. Maybe he was just embarrassed for being so mushy.

She put the phone on her nightstand and lay back. Mavis thought about his words, the ones about not hiding. Little did he know she was hiding all the time. Hiding her food, her feelings, and her thoughts. She was even hiding her skin. When she thought about these facts she didn't feel like a strong person at all; she felt like a hypocrite and a liar.

Mavis shook her head hard to try and clear it. She wasn't going to get down on herself. Whatever she was hiding, she was doing it for her own good, and the good of everyone who cared about her. She wouldn't have people worrying about her health or state of mind when she felt strong and healthy, and overall her mind was clear.

With determination, she thought about other things. She thought about the dance Saturday and made sure her timing would be right to attend the game and get home in time to change for the dance. She wouldn't be able to do it at school, like most of the girls who would take their dresses. Mavis wouldn't let anyone see the increasingly dark streaks of veins that ran through her white flesh.

Just something else I'm hiding, she thought to herself as she finally fell asleep.

CHAPTER 21

Mavis woke early the next morning.

She got ready for school, her spirit light. She even made her own breakfast, letting her mother sleep in by sneaking into her room and turning off her alarm. Mavis ate four bowls of bran flakes, packed snacks in her bag, and left the house quietly to go to Kim's. She wanted to pick her friend up for a change.

Just as she suspected, Kim was surprised to see her at the door.

"What are you doing here?"

Mavis shrugged as she went into the house. "I thought since the dance is tomorrow and we both actually have dates, that we should spend as much time together as possible."

Kim was obviously pleased, smiling as she gathered her things to leave. "You were overwhelmed yesterday, huh?"

"Ugh," Mavis replied. "It seemed like every time I turned around someone was there to talk to me, or touch me, or just gawk. I couldn't even breathe."

They left and started up the street. "Mr. Pearson made an announcement about it, asking everyone to give you a little space since you had been through a lot. I wonder when Shanice and Candy are coming back."

Mavis realized that she hadn't told her, and she knew that Mr. Pearson couldn't legally tell anyone. "They aren't coming back."

Kim stopped. "What do you mean?"

Mavis grabbed her arm and started to pull her along so they wouldn't be late. "My mom and I got the restraining order, I told you that, right?" Kim nodded. "Well, because of the order, she is expelled. She's going to have to attend another school or something."

"Wow," Kim said. "Well, that's good. You don't feel bad, I hope. Those pains in the necks needed to go away."

Mavis shrugged. "Yeah, but they are just going to victimize someone else. Their hearts are bad, Kim. Really bad."

She quickly changed the subject, bringing up the dance and telling Kim that she would be going home to change. Jeff would be changing at school; then he would pick her up and bring her. After explaining that the reason was because of her pale skin, Kim understood.

"Are you just meeting Shawn?" Mavis asked.

Kim nodded, blushing and smiling. "Yes. He's going to pick me up outside of the second-floor girls' room."

"Are you nervous?"

Kim burst out laughing. "Obviously, what do you think? I've never had a date before."

"Well, don't let your nerves get the best of you,"

Mavis said. "It's gonna be great."

∞

They got to school, and Mavis had already braced herself for more of what she got yesterday. While there were those who said something as soon as they saw her, most just offered her a smile and a silent fist punch to the air. The attention ebbed drastically, and it was obvious that Mr. Pearson's message had gotten through fairly well.

For the first time in weeks, Mavis enjoyed her school day. She got back her personal thesis and book report for *Passage of Time*, with an 'A' on the report. Miss Hawkins didn't grade disciplinary assignments, but she wrote a long paragraph about courage and standing up for the underdog, and how proud she was of Mavis for doing so. In parenthesis at the bottom of the note, she wrote, 'The PB & J is forgotten'; Mavis had to smile at the woman, who was watching while she read it.

Every other class went smoothly as well. She even stopped in the office in between third and fourth period to request that she be moved from last-period phys-ed starting the following Monday because she couldn't participate without showering. She tried to wear a full sweatsuit, and shower after school, at home. But she wanted to get things back to normal as quickly as possible, and picking up Health and Hygiene instead was a good step.

In art class the students were beginning a new assignment: they were to paint a portrait of their own souls. Mavis found herself intrigued by it, and dove in head first. She had always been very good at art, and for a time had considered studying it in college. The assignment would give her an opportunity to do some much-needed soul-searching. Maybe if she could get what was going on with her on paper, she could sort it out much more easily.

But the highlight of her day was seeing Jeff and talking to him before they went to their last class. They leaned against the lockers and casually chatted, and Mavis wasn't uncomfortable at all. Perhaps her apprehension was about all the things going on in her life; maybe she had a bit of shame that had been stealing her peace. She wasn't sure, but it felt good to relax around him again.

Once the school day had ended, Mavis and Kim stopped at the Dairy Pop on their way home. They bought chocolate-covered ice cream in sugar cones, and they took their time, sitting down to eat it. They excitedly talked about the game and the dance. Mavis was going to get her hair done by Tudie at Royal Dos the next day, and Kim told her that she was going to join her, just to watch. Kim's Aunt Rita would do her hair; she was a cosmetologist who worked from home, and it was the perfect arrangement to have her do it rather than spending money at a salon.

At the end of Mavis' block, the girls went their separate ways, with plans for Mavis and her mother to pick Kim up after breakfast in the morning so she could go to Royal Dos with them. When they had stopped to say goodbye, Kim paused before leaving.

"Is something wrong Kim?" Mavis asked.

Kim shrugged. "I don't know if you'll understand what I mean, Mav, but it sure is good to have you back. I love you, you know."

Mavis smiled and hugged her best friend in silence. Soon Kim headed for home, Mavis just stood watching her until she turned the far corner from the park.

But she really wasn't sure if she was 'back' at all. She felt more like a 'new and improved' Mavis. She felt like maybe they would all see it too before everything was said and done. After all, for the first time in her life, she was looking outside herself. Two months ago, she would have never dreamed of interfering in a bully-fest in the girls' room; yet the other day she didn't even give it a second thought. It was as if the ability to do something like that had been inside of her all along.

She turned up her sidewalk and began to consider the flesh-eating thing, the raw-meat preoccupation. What was that, if she was better? Well, if she was going to be honest, she really didn't care what it was. To her, it was okay, as long as she never let anything happen like she envisioned it with the delivery man.

By the time she reached the front door of her house, she had pushed all of that out of her mind. Tonight was important: she had no homework, and she planned to pamper herself a bit. She was going to take some of her own money and go to Super Nails at the strip mall and get a French manicure.

Kim always kept her nails perfect. As a matter of fact, she did them herself, but they weren't professional, and Mavis wanted something as close to perfection as possible. Besides, Kim had homework so it wouldn't be feasible for her to go with Mavis. So, she would ask her mother to go with her; they could make it another 'girls' day out' together.

"Mom, I'm home!" Mavis closed the door and set her books on the entryway table so she could remove her jacket.

Jane poked her head out of the kitchen. "Mav! Hi, honey! Hope you had a better day today."

"I did, actually," she replied with a smile. "What's up with you?"

She made her way into the kitchen to see her mother preparing more summer sausage and crackers with cheese. "Making you a quick, iron-rich snack, of course. Feeling okay?"

"Amazing." She grabbed a cracker, topped it, and took a glass from the cupboard for milk. "Say, I have that appointment tomorrow with Tudie, you know. But I was wondering if you would want to go with me to Super Nails today so I can get a French manicure; I'll pay for it. I would just like your company."

Jane beamed. "I would love to! Fill your belly, and I'll go change into something other than sweats. Sound good?"

Mavis dove into the food while her mother disappeared into her room. It seemed her appetite was ebbing a bit, though it was still focused mainly on red meat. She didn't want to risk going into her room right then to have some liver. Mavis thought she would save it until later and enjoy it when she didn't have to worry about being caught.

"Okay!" Jane came into the kitchen, the smile still on her face. "Whenever you're ready, we'll head out." She put some snacks on a plate and sat at the table with Mavis. "So, not as much attention from the kids today?"

Mavis shrugged. "No, there was plenty of attention, I guess, but they stayed out of my personal space. I didn't confront Shanice or press charges to get attention. You know that, Mom. I just wanted her to know how it felt to be the weak one, like the kids she victimizes."

"I know, honey. But you do realize that some people never get it." Jane took a small bite of a cracker, chewed it quickly, and swallowed it. "Those girls likely are whining that you victimized them, you know. People like that never seem to get it."

"I know."

They polished off the cracker snacks, and Mavis listened to her mother tell her about her own day. Jane relayed a hilarious story about an acquaintance of hers named Dorothy that she played canasta with sometimes. It seemed the woman sneezed earlier that day in the middle of Bitman's Department Store and peed her pants, but she didn't get embarrassed. Instead, she laughed so hard that she also ripped the butt right out of her soaked britches, and she and Jane could hardly get to the car, they were laughing so hard.

"OMG, TMI, Mom."

Mavis and her mother were both cracking up at the

retelling to the point where they had tears running down their faces; it had to be one of the funniest things the girl had ever heard in her life.

∞

At Super Nails, Mavis and her mother both got manicures and pedicures; and, of course, Jane wouldn't let Mavis pay. While they were there, Jane texted Mavis' father and told him to heat up some specific leftovers out of the fridge for supper, if he didn't mind. Jane wanted to take her daughter out to eat, just the two of them alone.

So, after the nails, they headed to Corbin's Steak House, where they both ordered the works: T-bones, potatoes, corn on the cob, and huge pieces of cheesecake for dessert. They talked about school, Kim, and Jeff, and they discussed the fact that, while Jeff was very verbal about his affections, Mavis just wasn't sure about rushing into 'love.' Jane supported her in this, not pushing her just because Jeff was good-looking or motivated or polite. It meant the world to Mavis, and the pressure she had been feeling regarding her new boyfriend was unloaded during the hour they ate together.

That night, around eleven, Mavis was lying in bed with yet another movie going on her laptop. The house was quiet; her parents had turned in early because they had plans to do yard work in the morning together, and there wasn't a sound in the place but for the low droning of the speaker on her computer. But Mavis wasn't really into it; she was thinking about the dance, and Jeff, of course. She was also leaning over and tearing at her last piece of liver with her teeth. She was excited but a bit shy, and it didn't help that she was also a little nervous. The nervousness didn't bother her; it was normal, she knew. It was going to be fun, and everything was going to be fine.

It wasn't until midnight that she finally lay down to sleep, and Mavis was out nearly as soon as her head hit the pillow.

CHAPTER 22

Saturday started out perfectly enough, for what was supposed to be one of the biggest days of Mavis' life thus far, but unfortunately, it didn't stay that way.

She woke at eight and set about doing her face and getting dressed. Her parents were already outside; her father was trimming the hedges, and her mother was weeding her perennials and trimming her annuals. She watched them through the kitchen window while she ate raw sausages and drank milk, Mavis found the sausages to be very satisfying.

Her hair appointment with Tudie was at ten, so she left the house to meet Kim at nine thirty in her mother's car, as planned. Kim was waiting for her on the front step, scrolling through her phone. Soon, the two friends were off, gabbing excitedly about the day to come.

As far as her hair was concerned, Mavis didn't want anything too fancy. She didn't want it worn up, or too girly, but she wanted to be beautiful. Tudie did a wonderful job: she trimmed it, put highlights in, and swept it back on the sides, accentuating her face with little spiral wisps. She then told Mavis to go home and stay in, so it didn't get ruined, and she fortified it with plenty of hairspray. Mavis had Kim take a picture, and she posted it on her Social Media page.

Kim's appointment was at one, so Mavis drove her home so she could have lunch, and she returned home to do the same. Her mother and father were waiting anxiously to swoon over her, and rather than complain about it, she let them. After all, she had made them wait a fairly long time for this day.

Jeff called her just after two during a practice break. To remind her that kick-off for the game was at five, and then suggested that, right after the game, he dropped her at home, so she didn't have to walk. It would save time, and all he had to do was go back to the school and change for the dance. He would be ready in plenty of time to pick her back up, and it might even give them a few minutes alone together before they made an appearance. Mavis agreed to the arrangement.

Her parents told her that they would also be leaving around five, just as the game was starting. They decided to have a 'date night'; they would go to an early movie, then have dinner out together. It was perfect for everyone involved, and with each passing minute, Mavis got more and more excited.

At four thirty, Kim showed up at the door, and the two of them, sporting Westside gear in support of their team, walked to school together for the big game. The place was packed, but they managed to get some okay seats together, and they watched eagerly, wanting their dates to win with a vengeance.

The first half of the game had everyone worried,

though. By halftime, the score was thirteen to seven, and the Westside Wasps weren't looking too good. But after the short band show at halftime, everything changed. It was almost as if they had replaced the entire team; the Wasps luck seemed to turn around, and they wound up taking out the Midtown Mavericks from Cincinnati violently, with the final score being thirty to thirteen.

Jeff found Mavis and got her home in record time. The dance started at eight, and it was already seven thirty by the time he dropped her off. He would be back in a half-hour. He figured they would spend fifteen minutes alone, then they would make their fashionably late appearance by eight thirty. It was a perfect plan.

But that was just about when everything started to go terribly wrong.

∞

Once at home, Mavis did her makeup first, then dressed, focusing on fixing her hair, which wasn't too mussed. She ate a couple of raw sausages, then brushed her teeth and touched up her lipstick. Just as she was finishing, the doorbell rang; it was Jeff.

"You look amazing, Mavis," he said in a husky voice when she opened the door.

She blushed. "Thank you."

He gave her a modest kiss on the cheek. He didn't look so bad himself. The tuxedo he was wearing flattered his broad shoulders, and his hair was perfectly combed. He looked awesome, and she couldn't wait to get some good kisses in before the dance.

"Shawn's picking up Kim, right?" she asked.

Jeff nodded and pinned her corsage to her shrug sweater. "They are already there."

After he offered her his elbow, the two left for the dance. He tucked her safely into the car and got in himself. When their seatbelts were buckled, he turned to her.

"I thought we could just park in the woods right next to the school for a minute," he said. "as we never really get any time alone; is that okay with you?"

She nodded, and the two were off.

Within minutes the car was parked, and the two were all over each other instantly, and the incidents which occurred over the next fifteen or twenty minutes happened very quickly.

They began to kiss, kind of slowly at first, but it quickly escalated. Soon, Mavis was sitting on his lap, straddling him; Jeff had the driver's seat put back all the way, and he had it reclined. They were comfortable, and they were soon going at it hot and heavy.

But the cloud soon began to come over her.

Within minutes, the kisses, though they continued, meant nothing. She sort of picked up where she left off when Brian interrupted them at Zander Point: she began to trail her kisses across his cheek, and she began to tease his earlobe, nibbling. She was vaguely aware of his growing excitement, but it made no difference to her. Mavis wasn't interested in sex at all.

She continued with her teasing and luring, not even knowing what she was doing in her mind. It seemed, in her way of thinking, that she was doing nothing more than playing with her food, toying with her prey, and Jeff was falling right into it. He was breathing quite heavily now, and his hips were beginning to involuntarily arch.

That was when she bit.

She did to Jeff much the same thing she envisioned doing to that poor delivery man. Mavis sank her teeth into his neck hard; he didn't even make a sound. If she could have seen his face, she would have seen his eyes fly wide open instantaneously. His entire body went stiff, his back arching in pain and surprise. Then, Mavis ripped at his jugular with her teeth, and blood shot from his body, covering both of them.

She spent the next twenty minutes dining on her boyfriend, the one who had been adamant that he loved her. She chewed and ripped and made wet smacking sounds. There was no hesitation whatsoever; Mavis enjoyed her meal immensely, and she did it quickly and efficiently.

Soon enough, she was finished. She sat back with a long, satisfied sigh and wiped her mouth with her hand. She sat in the passenger seat with her eyes closed, covered in blood. Her ears were ringing, and she felt so alive and energized that it was almost as if she had been reborn.

Slowly, but surely, she began to come back to her senses.

Her eyes fluttered open, and she looked over at him, expecting to see his smiling face glowing at her.

But what she saw horrified her. Jeff was no longer there, just bloody bones and a blood-soaked tuxedo lying on the floorboard of the driver's side. Music was still softly playing, but she couldn't even register the song. Mavis screamed.

After a minute she began to calm herself. She had eaten him, and she hadn't even meant to. As a matter of fact, she had been fighting this very thing ever since her dress was delivered. But it was done, and now she had to figure out what to do.

She reached over him and turned on the dome light; she could see the lights of the school in the far distance and dismissed any concern about her scream being heard. Once the light was on, she looked around the car: lying across the back seat was the zipper bag Jeff's tux had been in… that would have to do.

Mavis began to put his remains quickly in the bag, along with his suit. She made sure not to miss anything. Next, she took a hanky out of her tiny handbag and poured water on it from a bottle from Jeff's cup holder. Using the dome light to see, she carefully went through the car and wiped away the bloody prints, because they would be hers and hers alone. She left the rest of the blood and didn't clean any more prints because she knew that, too, would be suspicious. Besides, the priority was to get rid of Jeff himself. When she finished with the bloody prints, she grabbed a book of emergency matches from his glove box and tucked them into her bra, and she shoved the hanky into the bag with everything else.

Once everything was packed safely in the bag, Mavis did a quick double-check of the car for anything she may have missed. Satisfied, she picked up the bag and took off into the woods. She was going to have to bury all of it, as deep in the ground as she could get it, and she would have to do it fast.

For some reason, she had no problem seeing in the dark at all, but that fact didn't even register in her mind. Mavis ran until she came to a gully; right alongside it was a pit in the ground between two trees. She looked at it, glanced around, and then threw the bag into the pit. She began to grab sticks and leaves, and anything else she could get her hands on. Mavis dumped the debris on top of the bag, then repeated the process countless times. She moved like a robot with a single programmed purpose: to bury the suit bag that held the bones and torn, bloody clothing belonging to Jeff Deason.

Mavis was well aware that simply burying the items would not be sufficient. His parents would report him missing, and the police would get involved. They would find the bloody car, and they would search the woods. With a quick look around to make sure no one was watching, she took the matches and lit one and threw it on top of the leaves in the pit. They caught right away, but she lit another anyway and did the same. She lit the entire book and dropped each match randomly into the pit. Finally, she added the empty book.

It was a major blaze in only seconds.

It took her just over thirty minutes. When she was finished, she didn't return to his car; she simply ran through the woods and took backstreets and alleyways all the way home. Mavis cut through her backyard and let herself into the house through the back door.

A glance at the kitchen clock told her it was nine-thirty. For the first time, she realized her cell was buzzing like mad in her purse. Mavis ran to her room and pulled it out: Kim was calling. She answered the phone, put it on speaker, and began to undress.

"What?" she said, her voice frustrated and sharp.

"Mavis, where are you guys?" Kim asked. "We've been waiting for you, and we were worried."

She groaned. "He never came," she stated simply. The lie came easily out of her mouth, and it surprised her that she didn't even have to think about it.

"Who never came?" Kim asked, confused.

Now Mavis was getting pissed. "Jeff! He never came! I don't want to talk about it!"

She finished undressing and put her robe on. A quick trip to the kitchen for a garbage bag and a pack of raw sausages came next. Mavis put her dress, stockings, shoes, shrug, and undergarments into the bag and tied it tightly, then she stashed it under her bed. She planned to take the bag out to the garbage can, along with the other trash from her room, in the morning.

Her phone started to buzz again, but she ignored it this time. Mavis didn't want any more questions; she was afraid she might slip up regarding her story. Next, she went to the bathroom, locked herself in, and filled the bath. One look in the mirror told her that she was literally covered in dried blood. It was in her hair and all over her face, streaked on her arms and legs, and even in her ears. She bared her teeth and saw bits of flesh buried between them. While the bath filled, Mavis brushed her teeth thoroughly.

Finally, she was able to sink into the soothing hot water. It was then, and only then that she actually had the time to think about what she had done. She had accidentally eaten her first boyfriend.

It seemed surreal, and she began to silently cry. What had she done? She loved him, and at that moment any doubts she had about her affection were gone. She had ruined everything! At that moment, Mavis was struggling terribly; she was deeply confused, and she hated herself.

A loud whimper escaped her lips.

"Mavis, is that you in there?"

Her parents are home! Mavis got control of her voice and replied, "Yes." Her voice was weak, and even someone who didn't know her could tell she had been crying.

"Are you okay? Mavis, let me in."

She paused. "I'm in the bath. I'll be out in a minute."

Quickly, Mavis took the soap and began to scrub at her body with the washcloth. The water around her was pink, but there was no serious blood anywhere since it had dried by the time she buried his bones and got home. Next, Mavis washed her hair, twice, then got out and dried with an oversize towel while the water drained.

She used her towel, which was black, to wipe the tub down, making sure that there were no signs of pinkish water anywhere in sight. Mavis double-checked the sink, toilet, and floor, and she finished just as her mother knocked on the door for the second time.

"Mavis! I'm really worried! Why aren't you at the dance?"

Without a second thought, she popped the lock and opened the door. She didn't have to fake being upset, it was blatantly obvious that she was. Her eyes were rimmed with red from crying.

"Oh, honey, what's wrong?"

Mavis fell into her mother's arms and began to sob once again. "Let's go talk," Jane said as she soothed her, and she began to lead her daughter into the main area of the house.

"No, I want to go to my room," the weeping girl insisted.

Jane backed up, still holding her, and turned around. "Okay, okay. It's going to be all right."

Once they were in her room and the door was closed, Mavis lay on the bed dramatically and hugged one of her pillows close to her. Jane sat next to her on the bed and stroked her hair as she wept.

"Honey, if I'm going to help you, you have to talk to me," she began. "Did he try something with you? Did he hurt you? I should have known it was too good to be true."

Mavis shook her head, then got her crying under control. "No, nothing like that, Mom. He never even came to get me after he dropped me off to change. He never even came back."

Jane was silent as she processed this. "Have you tried to call him?"

"No, and I'm not going to," Mavis spat. "He probably hooked up with some bimbo at the dance and changed his mind." She began to cry all over again.

For the next ten minutes, Jane sat and comforted her daughter, trying to come up with scenarios that would explain the panic. Perhaps he was in an accident; maybe he got violently ill. But even her mother didn't sound like she believed them. If any of those things were the case, the boy would have called, and Mavis told her adamantly that he hadn't called once.

After a bit, Jane left the room. When she returned, she had a glass of water and one of her sedatives. "Take this," she said, putting the items in her daughter's hand. "It will help you sleep. I told your father just so you know. I'm sure he'll want more details when I go out there."

Jane stood and helped Mavis to bed. "That may hit you hard, so lay down, okay?"

Mavis looked at her and nodded. "Mom, if he calls, or comes by, or you hear anything, will you wake me?"

Her mother nodded and kissed her on the cheek. "Get some rest, honey, and we'll clear all this up in the morning. I'm sure something must have happened. It will be fine."

Jane left the room for the last time, turning Mavis' lamp out as she did so. The girl lay in the dark, her heart hurting over what she had done, but her mind racing about the situation and how to stay out of trouble. She hadn't meant it! What was going to happen to her over this? What was happening to her? Who the heck ate people, anyway?

Her head began to swim, and her thoughts slowed drastically. Why hadn't she thought to call his phone? That might be an obstacle, but in her dazed, semi-conscious state she thought she could explain it away with embarrassment, shame, and anger. Yes, she thought she might...

And with that Mavis fell into a deep, dreamless sleep.

CHAPTER 23

The following day was to be more chaotic for Mavis than any before it in her entire life.

When Jane left her room after putting her to bed, she had gone out and filled Todd in on all the details that Mavis had given her. He had been enraged, which was highly unusual for the man. They got all worked up and proceeded to phone Max and Meg Deason, as well as Kim, who had attended the dance with his close friend, Shawn Maher.

Much to the Harveys' surprise, the Deasons told them that Jeff was not at home; the last they knew, he had gone to the game and dance. They had been at a company dinner for his father, and couldn't attend the game, but they were sure that's where he was.

Next, they called Kim, who reported to them that neither Jeff nor Mavis showed up to homecoming. Kim stated that she had called Mavis and her friend had told her that Jeff stood her up; she had been upset and angry. She gave them Shawn's number, and he said the same but added that he hadn't been able to get a hold of Jeff on his cell at all, and he had been trying persistently.

This sparked a bit of panic in everyone except

Mavis, who slumbered in a deep, drug-induced sleep, unaware of anything that was going on. Within an hour, by eleven-thirty that night, the police had been called, and an all-out hunt for Jeff Deason and his car was underway. The Harveys even joined in, locking Mavis safely in the house.

At dawn, emergency responders received a call from a cattle herder who lived on the other side of the woods from the school. He reported seeing a trickle of black smoke rising from the middle of the woods behind Westside High. Police and fire trucks were dispatched, and the source of the smoke was located. By the time they arrived there were no longer live flames, only a smoldering pile of ash, with what appeared to be human bones in it.

Jeff Deason's car was located approximately ten minutes later, and soon it was quickly deduced that the bones found in the woods were likely those of Jeffrey Deason.

His parents were hysterical and heartbroken. Though they wouldn't know whose bones were found until the lab did tests, they knew. The interior of Jeff's car was soaked in blood, and the boy was missing. He had never even shown up to pick his date back up after dropping her off to change for the dance.

It didn't take much at all for everyone to assume that some low-life killer had abducted the boy and killed him in the woods.

∞

Mavis didn't even begin to stir until nearly eleven

o'clock the following morning.

At first, it felt to her like every other morning, except for the heavy feeling in her heart and the dull ache that accompanied it. For several minutes, she simply lay there, content and warm. But then, the events of the night before came rushing back.

Mavis sat straight up, panic-stricken. She looked at the clock, and when she saw the time she remembered the pill her mother had given her. What was going on? Why was the house so quiet?

Mavis jumped up and ran out of her room with no concern whatsoever regarding the paleness of her face. She found her parents sitting at the kitchen table, just as they usually did on Sunday mornings. But this time it was different. There were no smiles, and they both looked as if they had been crying.

"Where's Jeff?" She asked immediately, startling them both. "Did you find him? Did he dump me?"

Jane and Todd looked at each other somberly, then Jane patted the table at Mavis' seat.

"Sit down, Mavis," she said in a low voice.

For the next half-hour, Mavis' parents told her all that had taken place since she had gone to sleep. She expected it; after all, she knew. But those facts didn't stop her from immediately going into hysterics; hysterics because it was all true, none of it had been a dream.

Mavis had eaten the first boyfriend she ever had. She cried and cried. Her parents simply attributed it to the boy's death. Mavis played up her genuine tears. She cried and sobbed about how she had been angry and hated him, how she thought he had dumped her, and now he was dead. It hadn't been his fault at all. She was so emotional that her mother, who simply couldn't bear to see her daughter break down, fed her another sedative and put her back to bed. She was out again in no time, and the fact was, she welcomed it. Mavis was terribly traumatized by what she had done, and she was confused and hurt by what was happening to her to have made her do such a horrible, grisly thing to another human being.

She didn't wake again until evening. There was no Grandma Cabot that Sunday and her parents would not be sending her to school the following day. Todd told her the police stopped by to talk to her about Jeff, and they wanted to interview her on Monday morning at the station. They thought if she could report as to his exact words and state of mind when he left her they might be able to trace his path and figure out what happened.

Mavis should have been worried, but she wasn't. They wouldn't blame her, and she knew it in her heart. Even if they did, she didn't care. She deserved the electric chair or lethal injection. She deserved to die a death worse than his.

She couldn't eat at all, surprisingly. Mavis wasn't sure if it was because of eating her boyfriend, or because of her grief that she had. Her mother tried several times to feed her, but she just couldn't. She felt like she was on a horrible roller coaster that would never stop. Maybe she was dead already, and this was punishment.

CHAPTER 24

"Miss Harvey, we know this is very difficult. Just take your time and tell us everything you remember. Don't leave anything out; even the smallest detail could help us identify and locate Jeff's assailant."

Detective Martin's voice was soothing and gentle. Mavis sat in an interview room at the same police station she had been at just days before when Shanice had attacked her, but on this Monday morning, both parents were with her. So was a female detective who introduced herself as Detective Stein.

Mavis nodded slowly, still a bit groggy from the sedative. "Where do you want me to start?"

Detective Stein spoke up, using a soothing, motherly voice. "Just begin with the game, Mavis. Take your time; we have all the time you need; there is no rush."

Mavis felt tears welling up behind her eyes at the memory of what she had done, and it didn't help that she was preparing to lie about everything. She would use her tears for her benefit; she plucked a tissue from the box sitting on the table, sniffled, and took a deep breath.

"Are you ready, Mavis?" Detective Martin asked

gently.

Mavis nodded, and he pushed a button on a tape recorder.

"Well, we had a plan," she began. "Kim and I were going to go to the game together. You see, she was going to the dance with Jeff's friend, Shawn, and I was going with Jeff. We were going to go to the game, then Jeff was taking me home to change for the dance before he went back to the school to shower and change himself."

"Why was he changing at the school?" Stein asked.

Mavis sniffled again, then blew her nose into the tissue. Martin held out a small metal wastebasket, and Mavis tossed the soiled tissue into it. He set it down closer to her while she took a clean tissue.

"Usually students change at the school," she said. "At least, traditionally. I couldn't, though."

"Why is that?"

She shrugged. "I've been sick with severe anemia, and I didn't want everyone to see how pale I am. I mean, you can sort of see my veins and everything, you know? Jeff was going to run me home quickly, then go back and get ready. He was supposed to come and get me when he was done."

Mavis sighed, and a tear ran down her cheek. Everyone patiently waited for her to continue. Her mother had her hand on her back and was gently stroking it.

"Anyway, he dropped me off; I remember he was all sweaty and his hair was messy." She smiled at the memory. "When we got to my house he said he would see me soon, and he loved me; that was the last thing he said to me. That's why I couldn't understand it when he didn't come. He was my first boyfriend; I thought he stood me up. I thought he was dumping me."

She began to cry in earnest, and Detective Martin stopped the tape. "Let me know when you are ready to continue, Mavis."

She nodded and blew her nose again. After taking a couple of minutes, she looked at her mother, who gave her a sorrowful smile and patted her shoulder. This was so wrong on so many levels.

After a bit, she nodded at Detective Martin, and he turned the tape back on.

"So, I got ready for the dance." She threw her tissue away and got yet another. "Then I waited. And I waited, and I waited, I just waited, but he didn't come." Her voice began to crack, and Martin poised his finger on the pause button again, but Mavis shook her head and wiped at her tears. "I couldn't believe it. My friend Kim started to call my phone, but I ignored it because I was embarrassed."

"Did you try to call him?" Stein asked.

Mavis shook her head.

"Why not, Mavis?"

She shrugged. "I was hurt, and pretty soon I was mad. I figured, why should I call him? So I could look like a beggar or a stalker? After all, like I said, I never had a boyfriend before; what if it had been a joke the entire time? It didn't seem that way; he had seemed so genuine, and he started telling me he loved me right off, but I couldn't reason out why he wouldn't come except for that he changed his mind about me."

Stein nodded. "I understand. Go on."

"That was it. I changed out of my clothes, and I cried for a long time." She paused and wiped at her eyes again. "Finally, Kim called again, and I answered just so she would stop. I told her what happened; I was so upset that I hung up on her. After all, she was with his good friend and teammate. How could she not know? At least, that's how I was thinking."

Mavis broke down again, and off went the recorder. It didn't take her long to pull herself together that time, though. Pretty soon she was able to keep going.

"That was really it," she stated matter-of-factly. "I decided to take a bath, and that's when my mom and dad came home, and I told my mother what happened. She couldn't believe it either. She gave me some medicine and put me to bed. That's it."

Stein sat back in her chair and crossed her arms over her chest. "Have you noticed anyone strange or out of place around you or Jeff, or even around your school or in your neighborhood recently?"

Mavis shook her head. "Not at all; at least, not that I've seen. Jeff was out of town until Wednesday. He went out of town for some family member who was having surgery, so we didn't see each other for a couple of days. Maybe he had, but I talked to him all the time on the phone, and he never said anything to me."

She started to cry again, but not so hard this time.

Mavis simply laid her head on her mother's shoulder and let the woman soothe her with her love. She felt horrible; even though she had been the one to do this dastardly thing to such a wonderful young man, she was still grieving terribly. Grieving that he was dead, and grieving that she had been the one to kill him.

Detective Martin spoke up. "You had an incident with a couple of girls last week, Mavis: Shanice Hall and Candy Wilkes." He was reading out of a file that Mavis assumed contained copies of the police report on the attack in the alley. "What was that about?"

"What does that have to do with this?"

He sat back. "We just have to cover all our bases. What was that confrontation about?"

Mavis blew her nose again. "Well, at school last week, my best friend Kim and I were going to the girls' room between classes. When we got there, Shanice had this other poor girl, Donna Reilly, backed up against the wall and was poking her in the chest, hard, over and over. She was calling her names and… it was awful, just awful! So, I sort of… intervened."

The two detectives exchanged a glance. "What did you do?"

"Isn't it in the report you have?" Mavis asked.

Martin nodded. "Yes, but we would like you to go over it again for the sake of this statement if you don't mind."

Mavis nodded. "I pushed her into the sink and asked her how it felt to be the victim. I told her I never wanted to see her treating anyone that way again, or she would have to deal with me."

"Do you make a habit of standing up to bullies, Mavis?" Stein asked.

Mavis shook her head vigorously. "No. As a matter of fact, that was the first time in my life I ever got involved in anything like that. I guess that day, with all I was going through with being sick and all, I just couldn't take it. I couldn't take watching poor Donna, who doesn't have the greatest life anyway, be pushed around by such a mean, spiteful… person."

"So, what happened next?" Martin continued.

She took a breath and another tissue, throwing the last away. "Well, Kim and I were late to class because of the incident, so we had to go to the office for a pass. When we got there, Shanice was in the principal's office crying and saying that I had beaten her up, when I hadn't. We just told Mr. Pearson the truth, and he called Donna in. She told him the story, and Shanice got two weeks' suspension, and I got two days, though he said he wouldn't have even given me that, the situation sort of forced his hand."

Stein was nodding and smiling slightly, amused.

Martin continued with the questions. "This sparked Miss Hall's anger?"

Mavis gave a slight nod. "Yeah. The next day, I walked to the market for a soda and some snacks; I have to keep eating because of my anemia. I mean, I'm hungry all the time. Anyway, on my way home I got close to the alley behind the Smiths' house; they live pretty close to us. They have a tall privacy fence, and

Shanice and Candy were hiding behind it in the alley. I didn't see them at all. Just as I got to the alley, they grabbed me and pulled me into the alley behind the fence and started to beat me up. They pushed, kicked and hit me, and I was outnumbered. I bit Shanice on the face; then some people on the street started to yell for the police. Candy took off one way, and Shanice the other. The cops came, took me to the station, and called my mom. That was when we pressed charges."

Detective Martin was writing furiously, jotting a few notes for his own benefit in his little notebook. "Do you think they could have anything to do with Jeff's murder?"

Mavis thought about the question. She wasn't going to blame them outright, but she wasn't going to defend them either. It took her a minute to put her words together.

"I don't know," she replied. "I mean, he was big and pretty strong. They would have had to really fight, or have a weapon, or something. That's a horrible thought; he had nothing to do with our fight. Why would they do that?"

Stein said, "Maybe to get back at you."

Silent tears crept down Mavis' face again. She couldn't believe the lengths she was going to just to protect herself. But those girls deserved whatever they got; they were evil.

She just shrugged and cried. "That's horrible. Just horrible."

Detective Martin stopped writing and switched the

recorder off. "I think that's all we need for now Mavis, Mr. and Mrs. Harvey. Mavis, you've been an amazing help; you're a very strong young lady. If we need any more from you, we will be in touch."

The two detectives stood, and Martin took the small recorder in his hand, along with the file and his notebook. "Now, if you'll wait here for a bit we will have this transcribed. Then we'll need you to sign the statement. It will take about a half-hour, is that okay?"

"Absolutely, detectives," Todd replied.

"Can I get you any more coffee or soda while you wait?" Stein asked.

Mavis shook her head, but her parents went for the coffee, and the two detectives left the interview room.

Jane hugged her daughter tightly. "You are so strong, Mav. You did a wonderful job. I'm so sorry you are going through all this, and I love you."

"I love you too, Mom."

Just like that, Mavis' police interview regarding the murder of Jeffrey Alan Deason was over.

CHAPTER 25

Mavis was feeling a bit depressed, and more than a little confused.

As a matter of fact, the girl was beside herself with confusion. It was the confusion that was affecting her mood and emotions the most, not the loss of Jeff or the lies she told. She knew what she had done, and she missed him and grieved, but that wasn't what was breaking her heart.

She didn't understand what was happening to her; she only knew it wasn't anemia.

After the police interview, her parents took her to eat at the Happy Kitchen. Her appetite was fine, regardless of her life circumstances. Todd and Jane simply attributed it to her anemia, and since they wanted her strong enough to deal with things, they focused on keeping her body fed and healthy.

When they got home, Mavis put the bag with her homecoming clothes into the bag from her wastebasket and tied it securely inside. She took it to the garbage can in the alley and threw it away, getting rid of the last physical reminders of what she had done. She wasn't trying to hide her crime; she wanted to forget it.

With that task behind her, Mavis relaxed a little more. She didn't want to hang out with her parents, and they understood. All Mavis wanted to do was be alone. She had a lot of thinking to do that they knew nothing about. So, she stayed in her room with her television on a music video channel and kept to herself. Todd and Jane gave her the space she needed, her mother coming to her room only to bring her trays of food and to ask if she wanted anything. She needed her head to be as clear as possible.

At six o'clock that evening there was another light knock at her door.

"Mavis, Kim is here. Do you want to see her?"

She thought about it for a second. If she shut her best friend out it would be more than suspicious, and that wouldn't do. It was best to be as normal as possible, or at least, as normal as she thought she would be if her story were true.

"Sure," she replied as she unlocked her door. Mavis opened it, and Kim walked in timidly.

"Do you two want sodas or snacks?" Jane asked.

Mavis nodded. "I could use a snack. Do you want a drink, Kim?"

"Sure," she replied. "Thanks, Mrs. Harvey."

Jane ducked out, closing the door softly, and Kim sat in the chair at Mavis' vanity. Mavis herself plopped down on her bed and sat cross-legged. They were silent until Jane reappeared with chips, dip, and two sodas. When she left, Mavis rose and locked the door again, then sat back down.

"How was school today?" she asked her friend.

Kim wiped the top of her closed soda can with her forefinger, using a slow, circular motion and shrugged. "It was weird, I guess. The whole place seemed like… you know. Like someone had… died or something. Ugh."

Mavis shook her head and popped her own can. She took a long drink and set it down on the nightstand. There was tension in the room, but she knew it was because Kim didn't really know what to say.

"You know," the girl muttered, "I love you, Mavis, and I'm really, really sorry about Jeff. If it's any consolation, Shawn says Jeff really cared about you. He would never want you to think otherwise."

Mavis only nodded, then said, "Did the police talk to you?"

She nodded. "Yeah, but all I knew was that, after he got showered and changed, he said he was going to get you, and you'd be back in a bit. Whoever hurt him did it after he left, obviously. They asked me a lot of questions about Shanice Hall and Candy Wilkes, though. It almost seemed like they think those two had something to do with it."

"Yeah," Mavis replied. "That's the impression I got, too. I should have killed that Shanice when I had the chance. I should have bashed her brains in on the bathroom floor."

Kim didn't reply at all; she knew she would probably feel the same way if she were Mavis. "Look, Mav. I know you are going to need some time alone, you know, to think things through and get over this. I just wanted you to know that I'm here for you, always."

"I know that, Kim."

The girl stood and put her soda on the vanity, walking over to Mavis and giving her a tight hug. "Well, I'd better get going. Call me, okay? Whenever you're ready."

"Of course."

Kim left, and Mavis locked the door behind her. She plopped back down on the bed and lay back, staring at the ceiling. She wouldn't be able to hide away forever; she would have to figure out what was going on, or at the very least, learn to live with it in a way that wouldn't endanger others. The issue seemed to be growing rather than improving, and she couldn't just curl up and die.

She was going to have to get strong and buck up.

∞

In reality, Mavis spent nearly two weeks turning all of the circumstances of the last month-and-a-half over in her mind.

At last, she came to one conclusion: she wanted meat, and she wanted it all the time.

She knew that this desire was the sole reason that Jeff was dead. She also knew that she didn't want to hurt anyone else. The one thing that seemed to satisfy her at all, even though it was short-lived, was raw liver.

So, Mavis formed a plan. When her parents were gone one day about six days after the police interview, Mavis got another cooler, a larger, camp-sized one from their basement. She visited the market and bought all the liver in the store, including chicken liver, pork liver, and beef. She filled the cooler and packed it with ice. She used the little cooler to take some with her when she returned to school, which would be exactly two Mondays from the interview; as her mother kept her home for two weeks.

With all of that planned and arranged, she took the remaining free time to test her theory. Whenever she smelled another person and wanted to bite them, which was occurring more and more, she would go to her room and eat some liver. If she and her parents were out, she would dig some warm liver out of her purse, which she kept in a baggie, and eat that. It worked, for only short amounts of time. She would need to continue to keep stocked up. If she didn't want to hurt anyone else, it would be a constant job.

On Sunday, the last day she had before returning to school, Mavis sat alone in the backyard, a blanket over her legs and a jacket on, watching the moon and stars. Her parents had gone to Grandma Cabot's and wouldn't be home until later, but she had ducked out of the visit. She told them she needed the time alone to mentally prepare for school the following day, and they agreed.

As she sat there, Mavis thought about Jeff, and what she had done. Making out with boys simply wasn't going to work. When she got that close when she could smell them so strongly with her nose and taste them with her tongue, she lost it, and she knew it. She decided then and there that she would avoid being alone with boys at all costs, at least until she got this thing completely figured out, or until it went away, whichever came first.

Mavis smiled up at the twinkling sky; she would control it, and she would live without hurting anyone. She would adapt for the time being. This thing would heal itself. She was sure of it.

Mavis seemed to have it all figured out.

ENTREATY

This book was made possible by reviews from readers like you. Reviews fuel my creativity. If you enjoyed this novel, I implore you to please write a review and share your experience on the retailer's website. The livelihood for authors is entirely dependent on reviews, and I must say, it is the largest obstacle as a struggling author that I have encountered. Please tell a friend, tell a loved one about this read. With your help, I will be one step closer to overcoming this obstacle. In return, I thank you from the bottom of my heart, and sincerely appreciate your time and effort.

Humbled, with gratitude,

R.W.K. Clark

ABOUT THE AUTHOR

I am a father of two beautiful children, Jon and Kim. They are my motivating forces; they are the lighthouse in this vast ocean. In my life, they are the air that I breathe; they are the oasis in this desert of uncertainty. They are my greatest joy in life and my number one priority. I have a long list of hobbies, and I attribute that to my lust for life! I like to surround myself with positive people, who share the same interests. Family values, the arts, outdoors, nature, and travel are tops on my list. I embrace attending cultural and artistic events because I believe dramatic self-expression is the window to the soul. I wear my heart on my sleeve, and I still believe in chivalry, and I always treat people the way I want to be treated.

www.rwkclark.com